LEGENDARY

Retold by
Dan Green

Illustrated by
David Lyttleton

WeldonOwen
PUBLISHING

WeldonOwen

First published in Great Britain by
Weldon Owen Limited
Deepdene House
Deepdene Avenue
Dorking RH5 4AT, UK

Copyright © 2015 Weldon Owen Limited

Design: Jo Connor
Additional design: Natasha Rees
Editors: Fay Evans and Clare Hibbert

ISBN 978-1-78342-046-9

A CIP catalogue record for this book is
available from the British Library.

Printed and bound in China

1 3 5 7 9 10 8 6 4 2

www.weldonowen.co.uk

Weldon Owen Limited is part of
the Bonnier Publishing Group
www.bonnierpublishing.com

CONTENTS

INTRODUCTION

The book you hold in your hand is something special.
It contains extraordinary stories – some of them
thousands of years old. This is your gateway to an
amazing world, filled with outlandish creatures and
astounding happenings.

What are myths and legends? Myths and legends are just the most
awesome stories ever, and they are a big part of every culture in the
world. These epic, magical tales help us to explain the "big things",
such as life, love, death, creation, why society is the way it
is – and even the weather!

All stories die if they are not told. Telling myths and legends or writing
them out passes them down through the generations and keeps them
alive. They can also be told through dances, songs, paintings, and rituals.
Some people travel the world collecting local tales.

Many of these stories star non-human beings. Gods and goddesses are
more powerful than us, so stories about them help us to explain things
that we can't understand. Monsters, on the other hand, represent our
deepest, darkest fears. These beasts lurk in the dark, waiting
to gobble us up!

Many myths mix fact and fiction. Take the story of King Minos of Crete,
for example – archaeologists have dug up a palace at Knossos on Crete...
Could it have belonged to the mythical King who kept a
pet minotaur in a maze?

FiRE OF THE GODS

THE GODS WERE BORED. The wars between
the Titans and Olympians were over. "Being an
IMMORTAL sucks!" moaned Zeus. "Life is dull when
you're indestructible." Then, an idea hit him like one of
his **THUNDERBOLTS** – the gods needed something
to look after. Someone had to make some creatures,
and Zeus knew the perfect pair of chumps...

PROMETHEUS and his brother Epimetheus were Titans, but
they'd fought on the side of the Olympians in the wars. Zeus didn't
fancy socializing with this pair of losers, so he dropped off a sackful
of special **POWERS** and left them to it. Epimetheus got down to it,
humming tunelessly as he crafted his creatures from clay – digging
into Zeus's bag to give each one a gift.

When Zeus returned, he was impressed. There was a lovely logic to the lunkhead's work. Epimetheus had shared out the skills so that each animal was equipped with what it needed to **SURVIVE**. The big ones had sharp **CLAWS** and teeth; the small, tasty ones had been given caution and speed. The trouble was that Epimetheus had used up everything in the sack by the time he came to his last creation: **HUMANS**. They were left naked and **DEFENCELESS**. "Ho ho!" boomed Zeus. "These ones won't last five minutes!" But he hadn't counted on Prometheus. Not wanting his brother's handiwork to go to waste, Prometheus decided to make the humans as **INTELLIGENT** as gods.

Life did well on Earth and the gods were happy. Whenever they felt that old fed-up feeling coming on, they livened things up with a little flood or an entertaining natural **DISASTER**. It was tough for the humans, though. "Hey, we're cold without any fur," they complained (because they could speak now). So, although Zeus had expressly forbidden it, Prometheus stole **FIRE** from the gods' hearth, brought it to Earth and taught the skinny creatures how to make it.

Back in the heavens, the **DELICIOUS** smell of cooking meat rose to Zeus's nose. Looking down, he saw cheery fires with people gathered around them, chatting, eating hot food, and hanging out. The sight made Zeus as **MAD** as a tiger in a tutu! To punish Prometheus, he chained him to a rock. Each night, an **EAGLE** came to the rock and pecked out Prometheus's liver. The next day his liver regrew and the **TORTURE** began all over again. Despite the endless agony*, Prometheus couldn't help chuckling to himself when he thought about how he had stolen the fire of the gods – and got one over on the mighty Zeus.

* (IT WASN'T REALLY ENDLESS BECAUSE PROMETHEUS WAS LATER SET FREE BY HERCULES.)

DISH OF THE DAY: LIVER

GORGON, MaKe MY DaY!

YOUNG PERSEUS FOUND LIFE DIFFICULT and confusing. His mother was poor and his father, the god Zeus, was never around. Now **SLEAZY** King Polydectes had his eye on his mum. Some days it seemed like Percy versus the world. Little did he know that he was about to become one of the greatest **HEROES** ever!

Perseus was in trouble. At a fancy dinner at the palace, he'd promised to deliver the head of **MEDUSA** to King Polydectes. The other guests had pledged "ordinary" gifts, such as horses and gold, but Perseus couldn't afford all that stuff. Besides, he wanted to be **DIFFERENT**. He'd done it now. Medusa was one of the Gorgons – three foul and scaly monsters with poisonous **SNAKES** for hair, wild boar's tusks, and spiny wings.

They were a gorgeous lot, alright! A slow, sly grin spread across the king's face. "What a delightful offer," he said smarmily. "Don't let me delay you a moment longer – you'd better get going!"

How Perseus wished he'd kept his trap shut! He didn't even know where to find the Gorgons. The gods, always eager for entertainment, were amused by this **COCKY** kid and decided to lend a hand. Zeus gave his son a cool sword, while Athena dropped by with a shiny **SHIELD** and a bit of free advice. "Don't look Medusa in the face," she said. "She's so ugly, one look turns you to **STONE**!" "Oh great," thought Perseus. "This just gets better and better!" "Oh, and visit the **GREY WOMEN**," the goddess added. "They're the sisters of the Gorgons, and sisters always know each other's weak spots!"

The Grey Ones were three old **CRONES** who shared one eye and a single tooth between them. "Who's coming? Who is it?" demanded the first as Perseus approached. "Calm yourself. It's a nice young man," answered the second Grey One. "Let me see! Let me see! Give me the eye!" **CACKLED** the third. "OK. Swap you for the tooth," offered the second. "I've still got some leftovers from lunch to nibble at."

As the eye changed hands, Perseus darted forward and plucked it away. The **HORRID** threesome shrieked like seagulls. "Give it back! Give it back!" "Not until you tell me how to defeat Medusa the Gorgon," bargained Perseus. Well, of course they told him everything, including how to find the **NYMPHS** who would kit him out for the journey.

Everyone knows that nymphs love a **HERO**. These ones made Perseus feel like a real fighter! They gave him a magic pouch, **WINGED SANDALS** from the god Hermes, and a helmet of invisibility. The sandals took him far across the oceans until finally he arrived at the dreaded island of the Gorgons. The frozen stone bodies of other adventurers stood all around like **STATUES** made by some mad artist. Eventually he reached the cave where Medusa and her sisters lay sleeping.

Perseus headed straight for the **MONSTER**, but he knew better than to look at her directly. Instead, he used Athena's shiny shield as a mirror and looked only at Medusa's reflection. Her horrible hair was writhing and **HISSING**, but the hero kept his nerve and strode confidently on. With an almighty swipe he swung his sword and struck Medusa's head from her body. She let out a terrible cry that woke up her two sisters. It was time to skedaddle!

Perseus thrust Medusa's head into the pouch so he wouldn't look at it by accident – and then crammed his own head into the **INVISIBILITY HELMET** so that the Gorgons couldn't look at him. It worked, and he vanished into thin air. Once he was well away, Perseus took off the helmet and became visible again. As he flew, drops of Medusa's **BLOOD** splashed to the ground and wherever it fell, poisonous snakes sprang up. Hero he may have been, but Perseus also bears the blame for bringing snakes to Earth.

Percy made it home just in time to **SAVE** his mother from Polydectes' clutches – his flying sandals sent him skidding on the polished stones of the throne room! Certain that Perseus would never return, the king was unpleasantly surprised. His lip curled with **DISDAIN**.

"Surely you're not back with my gift already?" snarled Polydectes. "I surely am, your majesty!" said Perseus. "Feast your eyes on it!" Looking away and shielding his mum's face, he drew out the Gorgon's **GRISLY**, dripping head. Polydectes and his fawning courtiers were instantly turned to stone!

I AM HERE

THESEUS AND THE MINOTAUR

IF YOU PLEASE, spare a thought for the **MINOTAUR**. Because no one ever does – it's always about the bad temper and the even worse body odour. The poor thing meant no harm, he was just – well – a little **BULLISH**. Half-man and half-bull, the Minotaur was never going to be a looker. When it was only little, the bullboy was locked in a fiendish underground maze. Pitch-black and twisted, the **LABYRINTH** became the Minotaur's soul-crushing prison. And being given **HUMAN FLESH** to eat... honestly, it was never going to end well!

Every seven years, King Minos of Crete (who built the Labyrinth and chucked the Minotaur inside) demanded a **TRIBUTE** of seven strapping lads and seven pretty girls from the city of Athens to be fed to his stepson. Yes, you heard right, the Minotaur was his stepson. So this is where our wannabe hero, **PRINCE THESEUS**, enters.

Sick of Minos' bullying, Theseus volunteered as one of the Minotaur's man-snacks. His Dad, Aegeus, king of Athens, was not happy. He pleaded with his son, but all Theseus could think of was his glorious future as a hero. He jutted out his chin (to show off his lovely square jaw), looked off into the distance with misty eyes and said, "Dad, it's something I gotta do." "Every day, I will look out from the cliffs for your return," said sad King Aegeus. "If you defeat the Minotaur, use white sails – I will know you've won and I'll throw you the best party ever. If your ship bears black sails, I will know I have lost my only son." So with DOOM-LADEN black sails, the ship left for Crete.

At King Minos' palace, Theseus and the other tributes were treated well. The food was **AMAZING** and there was dancing every night, but each day their numbers reduced by one. Theseus felt ever more **NERVOUS**. Try as he might, he could not think up a plan to defeat the fearsome Minotaur.

Minos' daughter, **PRINCESS ARIADNE**, made things a bit more bearable. She was totally taken with the dishy prince. "You're so brave," she whispered in his ear as they danced (and boy could he dance!). Yes, things weren't too bad for our young prince. Mind you, no matter how finger-licking the food or fancy the dancing, the bellowing, **CRUNCHING**, and **SCREAMING** coming from the Labyrinth was kind of off-putting.

The night before Theseus was to be thrown into the Labyrinth, the prince **FRETTED** and **FUSSED**. Ariadne found him pacing the courtyard waiting for a bull-beating brainwave. "Hey!" she hissed. "I've put a ball of **GOLDEN TWINE** at the entrance to the maze." The prince blinked his puppy-dog eyes. "It's so you won't get lost." Theseus blinked again. "Tie the string to the door post and follow it back, silly! Otherwise you'll never find your way out."

Ariadne also gave Theseus a **BRONZE SWORD**. "Dad will go berserk if he finds out I've helped you," she said. "But you're so strong you'll beat the Minotaur for sure. And then you can take me with you and we can get married." she swooned. Theseus smiled to himself: I get to kill a **COW-MONSTER** and steal a princess at the same time. How cool is that? Ariadne led him down to the gate. "Remember: go forwards, always down, and never left or right," she said, "and come back safe to me." Theseus looked all cool and moody just for her, and ducked inside the Labyrinth.

Clearly the Minotaur hadn't washed in years. That place smelled **FUNKY**! Moving as silently as possible, unwinding the string as he went, Theseus melted into the **BLACKNESS** of the Labyrinth. He gripped his sword tightly – somewhere in this maze a very angry, very large man-beast was waiting.

Theseus melted into the **BLACKNESS** of the Labyrinth. He gripped his sword tightly – somewhere in this maze a very angry, very large man-beast was waiting. The maze was so quiet that all Theseus could hear was his pounding heart. He nearly screamed like a sissy when he walked **SMACK** into the sleeping monster! The Minotaur leapt up, let out a bowel-loosening bellow and charged. So much for the element of surprise!

The brute was on top of him in a flash. Its forearms were huge and hairy, and the blasts of its foul **BULL-BREATH** were enough to turn milk sour. Theseus fought back with all his might. The **BATTLE** was epic – it was just a shame no one was there to see it! Somehow Theseus got the upper hand and, taking the bull by the horns, he drove his sword into the mighty beast and killed it. **WOOHAY!**

Finally, a wobbly Theseus emerged from the Labyrinth with the Minotaur's head in his arms. Oh boy, King Minos was **NOT** going to take this well! "My lovely hubbie!" fluttered Ariadne, unable to take her eyes off Theseus, even though he was dripping in muck, **GORE** and **BULL BLOOD**. Theseus looked at her. He felt great! But guess what happened next! Theseus – hero, heartbreaker – did a runner, leaving poor Ariadne behind.

In his haste, however, Theseus **FORGOT** to change his sails. On lookout outside Athens, King Aegeus spied the returning boat... But... oh disaster! Oh despair! **BLACK SAILS!** Believing his son to be dead, the king threw himself from the cliffs. So with the Minotaur, a heartbroken Ariadne and his father no longer in the picture, Theseus finally became the hero he always knew he would be. What a **LEGEND**.

Jason and the Golden Fleece

HALITOSIA: **WELCOME** to another broadcast of **HERO QUEST.** Today we catch up with the exploits of the hero Jason as he embarks on a real-life **MISSION IMPOSSIBLE**. Let's go over to our reporter Smellios, live on the quayside at Iolcus. Smellios, what's happening down there?

SMELLIOS: Thanks, Halitosia. Wow, what a week it's been! When Jason limped into King Pelias's court wearing just one sandal we all thought he was a crazy **TRAMP** but, of course, he turned out to be ex-king Aeson's son – the legitimate **HEIR** to the throne, no less!

As we revealed exclusively on this show, Jason has been raised in the hills by a... by a... man-horse...

HALITOSIA: I think the word you're looking for is "centaur"?

SMELLIOS: Thank you! Yes, after years of training with the centaur **CHIRON**, Jason was returning to claim his birthright. Well, we were still reeling from that news when we began to hear **RUMOURS** from the royal palace that King Pelias was ready to give up his kingdom, on the condition that Jason brought back the **LEGENDARY** Golden Fleece.

HALITOSIA: But the Golden Fleece is the stuff of **FAIRYTALES**, isn't it?

SMELLIOS: So most right-minded people thought, Halitosia. But Pelias and Jason believe the fleece of the fabulous **FLYING RAM** really does exist. And Jason has agreed to go and fetch it. He must be genuine hero material.

HALITOSIA: Or else he's utterly **BONKERS**! So, what's happening now, Smellios?

SMELLIOS: Well, I'm here at the docks where Jason's boat, the Argo, is nearly completed. The goddess **ATHENA** made an appearance yesterday to bless the craft and give it a prow made of so-called "living oak". There was some confusion about what "living" wood could be until... erm... the boat began to talk!

HALITOSIA: Pardon?

SMELLIOS: Yes, you heard me correctly, Halitosia! The Argo is alive and can speak – it's the world's first **TALKING SHIP**! With Athena's help, Jason has put together an all-star crew. Never before have so many **HEROES** been assembled for one quest. There's the great Perseus, who slayed the Medusa; Poseidon's son Euphemus, who can run so fast across water that his feet stay dry; super-strong Heracles; Atalanta, the **WILD GIRL**; the Wind Brothers, Calaïs and Zetes; and Orpheus, the musician to the gods, to name just a few! I'm excited because I am joining these heroes on their voyage! I'll be your embedded reporter, keeping you right up to date. Back to you in the studio, Halitosia.

HALITOSIA: Welcome to **HERO QUEST** and what you've all been waiting for – a catch-up on the exploits of Jason. Are you there, Smellios?

SMELLIOS: Good afternoon, Halitosia!

HALITOSIA: Good to see you again, Smellios – we weren't sure we would!

SMELLIOS: After what we've been through, I'm surprised we made it this far. I'm coming to you live from the lands at the very edge of the known universe – **COLCHIS**, the kingdom of King Aeëtes.

HALITOSIA: OK. Tell us all about your **ADVENTURES** so far.

SMELLIOS: We've battled the **HARPIES**, made it through the fearsome **CLASHING ROCKS** by the skin of our teeth, and had many other hair-raising adventures.

And through every trial, there's been real team spirit! The crew are no longer a collection of individual heroes... they're now calling themselves the **ARGONAUTS**.

HALITOSIA: And the question we're all **DYING** to know – is the Fleece there?

SMELLIOS: I've seen enough dying on this trip, Halitosia! Sorry – yes, the most sought-after **PRIZE** of the ancient world is here.

HALITOSIA: So Jason has it, then?

SMELLIOS: Not quite. It's hung over a tree and guarded by a nasty-looking serpent. All Jason has to do is plough a field with a pair of fire-breathing bulls, plant the field with a **DRAGON'S TEETH**, and then defeat the serpent.

HALITOSIA: All in a day's work then?!

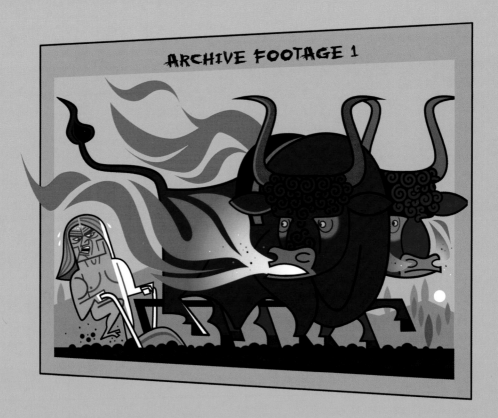

ARCHIVE FOOTAGE 1

ARCHIVE FOOTAGE 2

SMELLIOS: My sources tell me that Aeëtes's daughter **MEDEA** has taken a shine to Jason. She's a canny **SORCERESS** and might give the hero some magical help. Oh Zeus above! Jason is stripping off! Wow-ee! The buff braveheart is rubbing in some special cream... and it's working a treat! The bulls' flaming breath is just bouncing off him. **BRAVO!** Now, in go the dragon's teeth... Look out, Jason! They're springing up out of the ground as skeleton warriors!

HALITOSIA: Whoa there! Live broadcasts and handsome heroes are a fruity mix. I think we'll wait until that beefcake gets his togs back on. Apologies to any easily offended viewers. **PHEW-EY!** OK Smellios, tell us what's happening. What did we miss?

SMELLIOS: Simply **EXTRAORDINARY!** Jason made the warriors turn on each other. Then he gave the snake a sleeping potion that Medea had made. Once the serpent was snoring, Jason simply strode up to the tree and tugged down the fleece. The crowd is going **BANANAS!**

HALITOSIA: Marvellous stuff! Thank you, Smellios. Now all that you, Jason and the crew have to do is get back home to Iolcus! Good luck!

WE'D LOVE TO REPORT THAT JASON LIVED HAPPILY EVER AFTER, BUT THOSE CHOSEN BY THE GODS RARELY LIVE A LONG OR HAPPY LIFE.

A PRESENT FOR TROY

DEAR DIARY, It's dark in here. Thirty of us Greeks, the **TOUGHEST** of the tough, cooped up in the belly of this beast, trying not to make a sound. Diomedes says that if we sneeze, belch, or parp we have to make it come out like a horsey **WHINNY**! The Trojans mustn't guess we're in here. They've got to think that those "cowardly Greeks" packed up and shipped out in the middle of the night... leaving a **MASSIVE** wooden horse behind.

This is all **ODYSSEUS'S** idea. It's genius if you think about it – for ten long years we haven't come close to getting inside the fortress city of **TROY**, but now the Trojans are going to wheel us right through the front gates. There's a kind of poetry to that. From where I'm crouching, though, the whole thing seems barmy, bonkers, and utter baloney.

Honestly, the Trojans aren't daft – are they really going to believe the Greek army burned their tents and simply **SAILED AWAY**? Surely they'll guess that we're all hiding just out of sight around the headland? And are they really going to think this **HORSE** is a lovely present we've left behind? **NEIGH** chance!

I don't buy it and neither will Cassandra. She's the Trojans' soothsayer and she never sees the good side of things. She'll say, "**BEWARE** Greeks bearing gifts!" or something like that. One thing's for sure, we're in the hands of the gods – Poseidon, please make us brave!

Uh-oh, I'm going to sneeze...
Ahh... Ahh... Ahh... Oh. It's gone.

The gods have had their fun with us. They love a bit of war, and these last ten years they've had nothing but primetime battles on the plains. So much blood and so many men lost, and why? All because **HELEN** – Menelaus' wife and the most beautiful woman in the world – ran away with dishy Trojan Prince, **PARIS**. And where has it got us? Trapped in a jumbo-size hobbyhorse, that's where!

Shhh! Here they come...

DEAR DIARY, It worked! It really, really **WORKED**! I may have sounded a teensy bit doubtful yesterday, but of course I wasn't really worried, honest! I was just over-thinking things. That's always been my weakness – my **ACHILLES HEEL**, you might say!

It all went just as Odysseus planned. Talk about gullible! The Trojans didn't see anything remotely suspicious about a giant wooden nag parked outside their gates and **DRAGGED** us inside. We **LEAPT** out of the horse's belly like fire ants from a prank piñata. You should have seen the look on their faces. **CLASSIC**! It was the worst present ever!

We opened the gates to let the rest of the Greek army in and it was all over very quickly. It was goodbye and good riddance to Troy's royal princes and of course King **MENELAUS** got his wife back. But a good trick works only once, right? No one will ever fall for the Trojan Horse again. Or will they?

TO THE TROJANS, LOVE FROM THE GREEKS xxx

36

THE ONE-EYED MONSTER

"COME CLOSER, brothers and sisters! Let me tell a tale of my travels with **ODYSSEUS!"** Uh oh! Pappou was off again. My grandfather had been back from the war these twenty years, but the ten years he spent in the company of the greatest Greek **HERO** were still the freshest in his head. At any gathering the stories would come tumbling out. They always started the same way...

"Odysseus had streak of cunning. He was **STRONG**, too. He could eat three dinners in one sitting and fire an arrow straight through three axe blades. But he wasn't all belly and brawn – Odysseus had **BRAINS** as well. 'Try to win,' that's what he told us. 'And if you can't win fairly, cheat!' "

Pappou had fought in the famed **TROJAN WAR**. When it was over, he joined General Odysseus's crew, little knowing that the hero was **CURSED** by the gods.

If he hadn't made it home, I'd never have met my grandfather. As it was, I was only little when he came back with a bunch of outlandish and utterly exciting stories. I looked about the party. Some of the guests were throwing funny glances at each other, as if to say "Here goes that old **FOOL** again..." I tried to draw him away gently, asking if he wanted some more food or something to drink, but he was on a roll now.

"We landed on an island, **HUNGRY** and needing to restock, so we went in search of supplies. There was nothing special about this island – sheep here and there, that sort of thing, but it wasn't long before we found a **CAVE**, stuffed with all kinds of delicious meat, cheeses, and milk. We wanted to take it back to our ship and scarper as fast as we could, but Odysseus said that it wasn't the **RIGHT** thing to do. He was sure that if we asked the owner politely, he or she wouldn't refuse us.

"So we waited in the cave, and soon enough the owner arrived home. Oh! Sweet Aphrodite! He was a brute. Tall as a tree, he was, and instead of two eyes where yours and mine are, he had one huge, unblinking eye in the centre of his forehead. He counted his flock of sheep into the cave, then rolled an enormous stone across the entrance, trapping us inside. "Our ambassador – the one who always knew what to say – approached the cyclops. He was white with fear. Clearing his throat, he said in his best royal voice: 'Hello, um, good one-eyed fellow!' and then 'Give us some of your food.' 'Say please!' hissed Odysseus. '...Please.'

"The Cyclops grunted, plucked up our ambassador between his forefinger and thumb, and bit him in half. With his victim's legs still kicking, the giant crunched him up." Pappou stood rooted still. He had stopped talking as his story took him back to that cave. The room was so quiet you could have heard a porpai* drop. Then, in a shaky voice, he continued...

* A SHARP DRESS PIN, USED FOR HOLDING ANCIENT GREEK CLOTHES
IN PLACE. THE GREEKS WORE DRAPING CLOTH AS CLOTHES.

"We spent the night feeling very miserable, hiding at the back of the cave, while **POLYPHEMUS** – that was the monster's name – made the cavern shake with his snoring. The next morning, the Cyclops **GUZZLED** two more of the crew for breakfast and then went out with the sheep, closing up the entrance again.

"We tried everything that day to shift the stone, but it was no good. Meanwhile, Odysseus sat apart from us, deep in thought. By the time the giant came back that evening, he had a **PLAN**. He sauntered out into the middle of the cave as if nothing in the world could scare him and held out a **WINESKIN**. 'Hey Polyphemus,' he said. 'Why don't you have some wine to wash down your sailor tonight?'

" 'Wine?' exclaimed the Cyclops, with a greedy **GLEAM** in his eye. He snatched the skin and drained it. There was enough wine in there for six men. The Cyclops burped. 'Polyphemus like wine,' he slurred. 'Who are you?' 'My name is **NOBODY**,' said Odysseus. Oh, he was a man of many twists and turns. 'Ho ho,' went the giant. 'I save Nobody until last. I enjoy eating Nobody.'

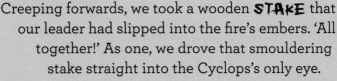

"But the giant was like a child and had no idea about wine and its effects. Before long, he was on his back, mouth wide open and **SNORING** loudly enough to wake the very gods from their slumbers. 'Now!' commanded Odysseus. Creeping forwards, we took a wooden **STAKE** that our leader had slipped into the fire's embers. 'All together!' As one, we drove that smouldering stake straight into the Cyclops's only eye.

"Well, that giant came up like a rabbit out of a fox den! Polyphemus's roars of pain brought other **MONSTERS** of the island to the cave. They banged on the stone door and asked if everything was alright in there. 'Nobody is hurting me!' the giant roared. '**NOBODY** has tricked me.' 'Sounds like he's gone crazy,' they said to each other. Baffled, they wandered off.

"To get out of that horror cave, Odysseus had to weave his **CUNNING** once more. Without Polyphemus to roll the stone we'd be trapped inside forever. In the morning, the blind giant started counting his animals, feeling their woolly backs as they trotted out of the cave. So, Odysseus roped each of us underneath a sturdy ram – gripping the thick wool, we made it out into the sweet meadows.

"You've never seen a crew set a ship to sail that fast, I can tell you! Then we made a **HULLABALLOO** taunting the Cyclops, whooping that his breakfast was escaping and calling him names that I'm too polite to repeat here. In blind fury, the giant hurled **HUGE** boulders into the bay as we rowed out – and a fair few nearly hit their mark! That was how we escaped the one-eyed giant."

The party guests were stunned. Here was a genuine hero in their midst – the type of character they sang **SONGS** about. My Pappou had travelled to places they'd never even heard about, and seen things they couldn't begin to imagine. But despite his wild adventures, he had made his own way back home. I looked at this old man and nearly **BURST** with pride. I loved him so much.

A MATCH MADE IN HEAVEN

THIS IS A RUN-OF-THE-MILL LOVE STORY:
immortal boy falls for a mortal girl and makes himself
invisible; girl learns to fly and travels to the land of the
dead to prove her love... Nothing exceptional, just an
ordinary, everyday tale!

PSYCHE was the youngest daughter of a standard-issue king and
queen, but she was a knockout – so beautiful that no man had the
nerve to woo her. Instead, dudes travelled for miles just to gawp at
how lovely Psyche was. Hopelessly ga-ga, the love-struck loonies
started **WORSHIPPING** her.

VENUS, the goddess of beauty, was mightily miffed when she heard this and sent her son Cupid to ruin the mortal upstart. Cupid was a **TROUBLEMAKER** whose arrows made folk fall in love. He thought it would be a hoot to make pretty Psyche fall for some ugly beast. But when Cupid saw her, everything changed. Stunned by her beauty, he dropped one of his passion-tipped darts onto his foot. He was instantly **SMITTEN**!

Meanwhile, Psyche despaired of ever finding a husband. Unaware that the **GOD OF LURVE** himself was all mushy over her, she took herself to a dangerous cliff edge. Before she could do anything silly, however, the gentle **WEST WIND** carried her away to a distant villa – acting on Cupid's orders, of course.

With the girl of his dreams installed in his pad, Cupid set about trying to win her heart. But **LOVE** does strange things and, for the first time in his life, the gorgeous god worried about his looks – especially his ridiculous **WINGS**! So, Cupid made himself invisible. Even though she couldn't see him, Psyche soon fell head-over-heels for this charming stranger.

Night after night, though, Psyche's **CURIOSITY** grew, until it was too much to bear. Taking a lamp – and a dagger, you know, just in case – she tiptoed around the vast mansion. When she found her shy guy asleep, she was blown away. He was perfect pin-up material – and what an **AWESOME** pair of wings! Just as Psyche leant in to take a closer look, Cupid opened his eyes. Seeing his beloved bending over him, dagger in hand, he cried out in fright and flew far, far away.

Poor Psyche was a wreck. **HEARTBROKEN**, she called out to Venus for help. Little did she know that Venus was Cupid's mum – or that Venus was still envious of her many followers. To win back Cupid, Venus advised, Psyche must bring her some of the beauty of **PROSERPINE**, the Queen of the Underworld. She "forgot" to mention that no one who descends to the kingdom of the **DEAD** ever returns.

Luckily Psyche wasn't just anyone. The strong-willed stunner went prepared. She made sure she had money for a return trip across the River of the Dead, as well as some cake to bribe **CERBERUS**, the three-headed hound that guards the gates of Hell. Psyche was back with Proserpine's beauty in a box in no time. But, again, curiosity got the better of her. Psyche couldn't resist taking a peep. Who knows what she saw, but it was so dark and **FOUL** that she was knocked out cold.

Sensing his soulmate was in trouble, Cupid flew to the rescue, but he couldn't rouse her. Luckily Jupiter, the king of the gods, knew **TRUE LOVE** when he saw it. He had a quiet word with Venus and gave Psyche a drink of **AMBROSIA**, making her immortal. Now Cupid and Psyche could be together forever!

THE ~~10~~ 12 TASKS OF HERCULES

MEET HERCULES! THIS HEAVYWEIGHT was a demigod – his mum was human but his dad was **JUPITER**, king of the gods. No task was too great for this heaven-sent handyman, but to prove himself worthy of becoming ~~IMMORTAL~~ like his father, Hercules had to pass ten tests – yes, ten – set by King Eurystheus. The only catch was Eury and Herc were deadly rivals. Eurystheus saw this as his chance to wipe out Hercules!

#1 LIQUIDATE THE LION

The first challenge was to defeat the biggest lion ever seen. This man-eater was no **PUSSYCAT** – spears and arrows just bounced off the beast's tough hide. Hercules tossed away his weapons, wrapped the lion in a **BEAR HUG,** and choked it. After **SKINNING** it with its own claws, Herc slung its hide around his shoulders. With his "signature look" sorted, the strongman sashayed back to Eury's palace.

#2 SLAY THE HYDRA

The next task was to kill the Hydra, a huge monster with many **VENOMOUS** snakeheads. The trouble was, every time one of its heads was cut off, another sprouted in its place. Boo **HISSSS**! Winning took teamwork – while Hercules hacked off the Hydra's heads, his nephew **IOLUS** burned the stumps with a flaming brand, stopping more heads sprouting. Once the monster was dead, Herc dipped his arrows in its toxic **BLOOD** – these would come in handy later. When Eury saw Hercules returning alive, his face turned chalk-white. "If this **GORILLA** can defeat the Hydra, just think what he could do to me!" worried the king. He had a big bronze "panic jar" built, where he could hide when Hercules came visiting.

#3 GRAB THE GOLDEN HIND

The graceful deer that lived on Mount Ceryneia was so **SWIFT** she could outrun an arrow – catching her wasn't going to be easy. After a whole year, Hercules finally trapped her but, as he slung the hind over his shoulders, **DIANA**, the goddess of hunting, appeared. "Where in Hades do you think you're going with my favourite golden deer?" she demanded. Hercules turned on the **CHARM**, begged forgiveness and promised to bring the deer right back. Diana blushed and let the dashing demigod go. King Eury's plan to get Hercules in trouble with the goddess was foiled.

52

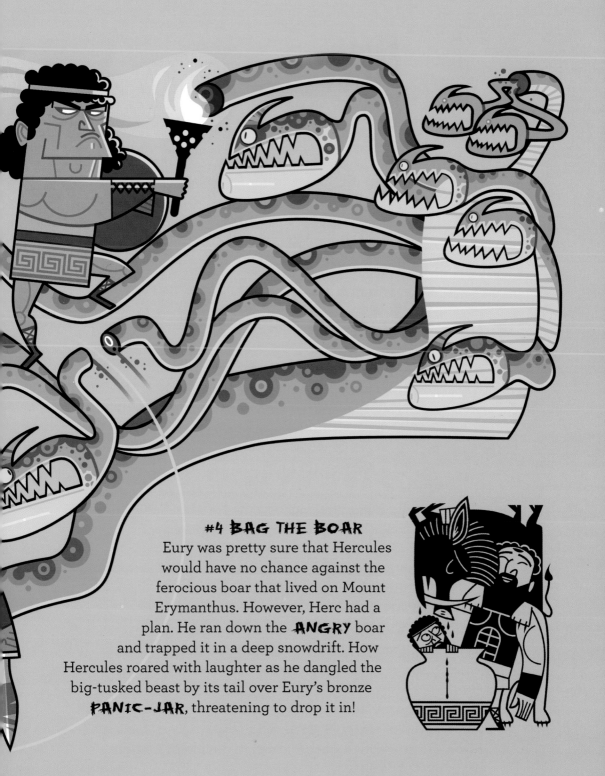

#4 BAG THE BOAR

Eury was pretty sure that Hercules would have no chance against the ferocious boar that lived on Mount Erymanthus. However, Herc had a plan. He ran down the **ANGRY** boar and trapped it in a deep snowdrift. How Hercules roared with laughter as he dangled the big-tusked beast by its tail over Eury's bronze **PANIC-JAR**, threatening to drop it in!

4 DOWN 8 TO GO...

#5 MUCK OUT THE STABLES

Three days later, lily-livered King Eury sent Hercules to clean out the Augean Stables. "Ha!" thought the hero. "This will be a **DODDLE**! The healthy life, fresh country air..."

– Hi! Hercules is the name.
– Where did you get that groovy **LION SKIN**?
– Actually, it once belonged to the Nemean lion...
– Ooooookay... So, what's it to be, Mr Hercules?
– I'm here to clean the stables.
– Oh, great! King Augeas owns more horses and cattle
than anyone else in the world –
– Zeus O'Reilly! What's that **STENCH**?
– Erm, we've been meaning to clean them out... It's just that
for the last, ahem, thirty years we've never got round to it.
– Thirty years of manure – **GROSS**! This'll take an eternity!

It didn't take forever, though. Hercules showed his smarts again
and rerouted two **RIVERS** through the stinky stables.
The filthy floors were washed clean in double-quick time.

#6 SLAUGHTER THE STYMPHALIAN BIRDS

Eury was getting tired of Hercules's hit rate, so he sent him to Lake Stymphalis. This idyllic picnic spot was rather ruined by the **FLESH-EATING** birds in the thick trees around the lake. Luckily, Hercules had a clacker from the goddess Minerva. Whirling it above his head like a crazy football fan, he startled the heinous birds from their roosts. After that, it was simple for **HOTSHOT** Herc to knock the flock from the sky with his poison arrows!

#7 TAME THE BULL OF CRETE

Eury figured it was not too late for one of his beastly challenges to bring about Hercules's downfall. He sent the demigod to Crete, where a **RAGING** bull was wrecking the island. The beast was the father of the monstrous Minotaur that Theseus had defeated. Heavyweight Hercules brought the brute to its knees in a bullish battle of brawn.

#8 HIJACK THE HORSES

By now Eury was a gibbering wreck. He sent Herc to his eighth task – stealing Diomedes's fine horses – without bothering to mention that the mares were trained to eat human **FLESH**! Under cover of darkness Herc crept into their paddock, but when one horse nibbled at his nethers, he raised a mighty **HOO-HAH**. Diomedes came running in his night-toga and Hercules fed him to his own horses. Then he led the full (and now rather sleepy) fillies away.

8 DOWN 4 TO GO...

#9 WIN THE WAR BELT

Next, Eury asked for the belt of Hippolyte, queen of the **AMAZONS**. The cunning king hoped that Hercules might cause trouble for the warlike tribe of women – and he wasn't wrong! Hippolyte was secretly impressed with the hero, so when he asked very nicely for the belt, she agreed. But the goddess Juno decided to stir up **TROUBLE**. She told the Amazons that Hercules planned to carry off their leader. When Herc saw a column of **ARMOUR-CLAD** women advancing towards him, he thought that Hippolyte had tricked him. It wasn't long before the Amazons lay twisted on the ground around him. Oops!

#10 RUSTLE THE RED CATTLE

Hercules's last task was to steal the giant Geryon's cattle. Geryon lived at the end of the world, and his cattle were the colour of the setting sun. Hercules's welcoming committee was snarling **ORTHUS**, a two-headed guard dog. With one swing of his mighty club, Hercules knocked the dog down. Then he gave the herdsman a sore head, too. Hearing the rumpus, Geryon put on his three helmets, strapped on his three shields, and picked up his three spears – this was no ordinary **GIANT**, you see. He had three heads, three pairs of arms, three legs, and even a pair of wings! Even so, Geryon was no match for Hercules and his poisoned arrows. Soon, the hero was heading home with the beef.

#11 GET THE GOLDEN APPLES

Hercules's ten tasks were done and dusted, but this supply of impossible gifts from faraway lands was too good to stop. Eury wanted more. The king passed some scribbled notes out of his pot... The first note said: "I've decided that killing the Hydra doesn't count, 'cos you had **HELP** from your mate, innit?" The second note said: "I don't think cleaning the stables counts either? You got the rivers to do the **DIRTY** work. So there!" And the third note said: "So I'm gonna give you 2 extra tasks, yeah? First, get me some apples from the Garden of the Night. Thanks."

Scrumping apples seemed easy enough, but no mortal could enter the mythical garden. Still, heroes don't quit. Hercules went to see **ATLAS**, whose punishment for fighting on the side of the Titans against the Olympians was to hold up the sky for eternity.

– Hi Atlas, how's tricks?

– **HEAVY**, dude.

– How about I take the sky for a bit,
you know, carry that weight?

– Are you sure? I mean, it's really heavy...

– No problem. Take a load off. Say, can you go get
some **DELICIOUS** golden apples?

<Some time later>

– Atlas, you're back! And you got the apples!

– **AWESOME**! I'd best be off.
I'll take those apples and you can have the sky again... Atlas?
– You know what? I'm kind of tired of holding up the sky.
– Cool. I'm totally cool with this, Atty. But could you just
hold it for a sec while I get a cushion for my shoulders?
– OK then. Hup!
– **SUCKER**! Thanks for the apples!
– Hey! Come back! Grrr! Wait 'til I get my hands on you!

#12 FETCH CERBERUS

Hercules's twelfth and final task was to bring back Cerberus, the
terrifying three-headed dog that guards the gates of the Underworld.
Herc went to **PLUTO**, the king of the Underworld, and asked him if he
could borrow Cerberus for a bit. It helps to have friends in low places!
Pluto agreed and, of course, Hercules soon mastered the mutt. The
drooling **HELLHOUND** terrified King Eury. "Please, please, please take
that dastardly dog back. I promise to release you!" squeaked the king.
And that was that – Hercules had finally passed the last of Eury's tasks
and proved himself **WORTHY** of being made an immortal.

HERC 12 – EURY 0

HAMMER
OF
THE GODS

DID YOU HEAR the one about Thor's **HAMMER**? Thor, the Great Norse God of Thunder, woke up one morning to find that someone had **STOLEN** his hammer. To say that Thor was terrible at taking a joke doesn't even begin to cover it, and this was exactly the kind of silly **STUNT** that Thor's brother Loki was always pulling...

Before he knew what had hit him, Loki was being held up against the wall by his brother Thor. For once, however, Loki wasn't to blame. Legs swinging, he promised to find the real culprit. It didn't take long – Loki soon heard that the **NOT-VERY-BRIGHT** giant Thrymr had been **BOASTING** about getting his big mitts on Thor's hammer. The weapon was so powerful it could flatten mountains with a single blow, and so special that it even has its own name: Mjölnir.

Loki turned into a falcon and flew off to have a little chat with Thrymr, but the **BULL-HEADED** giant wasn't falling for his tricks. Thrymr reckoned that with Mjölnir on his side, he and his fellow giants finally stood a chance of taking over from the gods. He wasn't going to give it up that easily. "Isn't there anything from the kingdom of the gods you'd like in exchange for the hammer?" tempted Loki. "**DIDDLY-SQUAT**," replied the giant firmly.

"Really? Are you sure there's nothing at all?" insisted Loki. Eventually Thrymr gave in. "Well," he blushed shyly. "I don't suppose you could get that pretty goddess Freya to marry me?" Loki promised he'd sort it out and off he flapped. There was no way in heaven Freya would marry a **DOLT** like Thrymr, but the clever trickster was already forming a plan.

Imagine the scene: with a little help from the lovely Freya, Loki dressed up Thor so that he looked like the goddess, **SQUEEZING** Thor's big, hairy body into a floaty bridal dress. "What a lovely lady you make! Who would have thought it?" Loki and Freya teased. "Grrrrr!" **GROWLED** Thor. He really was not happy with the situation, but he'd play along if it meant getting back his precious Mjölnir. Off he went to the so-called wedding, leaning on Loki's arm. "Stop stomping and keep your veil down!" hissed Loki as they entered Thrymr's castle.

The wedding feast was a **BLINDER**. Whatever his other failings, Thrymr certainly knew how to put on a spread! The "bride-to-be" couldn't help herself. She ate an entire ox, swallowed a net full of salmon and **GUZZLED** six barrels of mead. "Blimey," whispered Thrymr to Loki. "She's got a healthy appetite on her!" "Well, she's been so excited about marrying you, she hasn't eaten for a week," lied **SILVER-TONGUED** Loki.

The lovelorn giant forgot his manners and lifted the bride's veil to snatch a kiss... Surely the game was up! "My, what big **MUSCLES** you have!" The giant's eyes narrowed. "And so very hairy!" "Erm, yes," mumbled Thor huskily. "I've been so – erm – all-of-a-flutter, I forgot to shave."

This seemed to settle it for Thrymr. "Let's get this party started," shouted the giant, pulling Thor's hammer out of its hiding place to bless the marriage. "Yes, let's!" rumbled Thor, **BURSTING** out of his dress. Grabbing Mjölnir from the stunned bridegroom's fist, he started swinging it around and – quite literally – brought the house down! In the confusion, Thor and Loki escaped. You should have seen the look on those **DUMB** giants' faces!

BEOWULF AND THE SWAMP MONSTERS

THIS IS A STORY ABOUT ANOTHER TIME – now long past. An epic age of warriors, heroes, and barehanded combat with demon **MONSTERS**! This tale is blood-soaked and terrifying. If you have the stomach for it, this is how it went down.

BEOWULF arrived in the Land of the Danes as the sun was setting. He and his war party dragged the ship loaded with battle tackle up onto the sand. Take a look at the guy on the beach – anyone could see that this was no "hanger-on in hero's armour"! Beowulf was a **PRINCE** of Geatland. He was a really big Geat – a bear of a Geat – and he was really, really good at fighting.

Beowulf had arrived to help **HROTHGAR**, the king of the Danes. Hrothgar was an awesome hero-king – a jolly good rampager and ransacker, too – but he had a problem. He had built a **MEAD HALL** (a kind of olden-day nightclub) where they served beer and herring, and had loud parties with poetry readings and singing. If there was one thing the Danes enjoyed more than fighting, it was singing songs about fighting. Hrothgar's mead hall was a **ROARING** success until it began getting nightly visits from the wrong sort – **GRENDEL.**

Grendel was a huge marauder from another world. He had come from a place of demons, wolves, and **DARKNESS.** The singing and partying hurt Grendel's ears and made him mad. Each night the monster broke down the doors of Hrothgar's hall and crunched up some of the merrymakers. Now everyone liked a bit of **RANSACKING**, but this was too much.

Beowulf and his men settled into the mead hall. The night was young so the Geats began trading raiding stories with the Danes, telling of journeys they'd made and villages they'd **PILLAGED**. At some point, Beowulf took off all his armour, claiming it would give him an unfair advantage in a fight with Grendel. The partying went on late into the night but eventually the last raver was tucked up.

This was when the **SWAMP THING** chose to join the party. The watchman didn't stand a chance! Down came the front doors – again! – and Grendel was in. If his breath was bad, his bloody teeth, and crunching jaws were worse. This beserk **BEAST** wanted to cram as many Danes and Geats into his paunchy belly as he could.

With a **BLOOD-CURDLING** battle cry, Beowulf jumped on Grendel's back and the pair crashed around the hall. Beo got a hold on the brute's arm and, with a grunt, tore it from the socket. The swamp fiend went off into the night, **HOWLING** with self-pity.

Well, after such a successful fight, there was only one thing to do – have another party! But this time, who came a-party-pooping but Grendel's **MUM**! And boy, was she annoyed with Beowulf! Let's not make a big deal of it – Beo took a **BEATING**. It was mayhem. (In later years, Geat storytellers hurried over that part of the tale...)

Now, this was personal! The very next day, Beowulf took the fight to **MUM-ZILLA** herself. Clad in his armour, he rode to the marshes, and slid into the murky swamp.

He squelched his way along the bottom until he found the monster's stinking **LAIR,** full of the bodies of the innocent victims and brave warriors she had killed.

Shaking the clinging pondweed from his hair, Beowulf strode into the cave calling Grendel's mother all kinds of foul names. He needn't have bothered because the Old Girl was waiting for him. She pounced and pinned the warrior down. Beo's sword **SHATTERED**, and in that moment it was nearly all over. With Grendel's mum snapping at his face, the hero gave a last mighty heave-ho. Casting around **DESPERATELY**, he grabbed a sword from the gloomy hoard and brought it down hard, sending Grendel's mother to the neverafter.

The Danes loved to **PARTY** (did we mention that?). They dragged the exhausted prince out of the mire, carried him back to the hall and let it all hang out. Boy, they really brought the house down! There was gift-giving and long speeches – they even cracked out the house special: **ROTTED FISH**. Yum!

The partying went on for days, but **EVENTUALLY** it was time for brave Beo and his warriors to return home. Everyone came down to the beach and waved him off, his boat loaded with gifts and fishy treats. Back in Geatland, what **STORIES** they had to tell... and then there were the stories about the parties where the stories were told!

Beowulf had always been **KING** material, but now he had proved himself twice over. No one was surprised when he became king of the Geats. He ruled for a long time, but of course, once a hero, always a hero. If a silly fool steals a brooch from a **DRAGON'S** treasure stash, and then that dragon starts torching villages and burning the land, a hero has to ride in to save the day. You have to take a stand, even if your aching old bones would be better off relaxing in the bath with a mug of hot milk. So it was that old King Beowulf rode out to one **FINAL BATTLE** with the dragon – a battle from which neither he, nor the fire-breather would return.

Q: WHY ARE MEDIEVAL TIMES CALLED THE "DARK AGES"?
A: BECAUSE OF ALL THE KNIGHTS!

GAWAIN AND GREEN KNIGHT

IT WAS NEW YEAR'S DAY. King Arthur and his Knights of the Round Table were having a jolly time feasting and laughing at the jester's terrible jokes. It was young Sir Gawain's first visit to **CAMELOT**. Everyone was there: Arthur's favourite, Sir Lancelot, was showing off as usual; Sir Hector was lecturing everyone; Sir Cumference, the inventor of the **ROUND TABLE**, was doing the rounds; and Sir Prize wouldn't stop with his practical jokes.

Suddenly there came a loud knocking. **BOOM! BOOM! BOOM!** "Whoever comes calling at Christmas should not be turned away," said the king. "Enter, O Yuletide Knocker!" The door swung open and in rode a knight who was a vision in glittering **GREEN**. His armour was bright emerald. His shield shone a lovely shade of lime. His jade helmet was hung with olive tassles. Even his horse was green! More than that, he was **GINORMOUS**! The pea-green axe he hefted was the biggest the knights had ever seen. They were green with envy!

"I've come to test the **HONOUR** of the famous Knights of the Round Table," announced the mysterious Green Knight, his voice ringing out around the hall. "How about we play a little Christmas game?" he boomed. "Oh goody!" piped up Gawain. "I love games. Can we play Knighty Knight?" "Not Knighty Knight. This is a new one. I call it the **BEHEADING** Game." "What a funny name. How do we play?" The Green Knight explained – he would take a single **AXE BLOW** from any knight. "What's the catch?" asked Sir Spicious. "There's always a catch." "The knight must promise to take a return axe blow from me **ONE YEAR** from this day!" bellowed the green giant. Gawain heard himself say, "I'll take you on, you great green galoot!" "**HO HO HO**!" guffawed the Green Knight. Taking off his helmet to show his hairy neck, he gave Gawain a broad wink. "Strike well. You only get one chance!" Gawain lifted the massive axe and swung it with all his might. With a revolting sucking sound, the mysterious Green Knight's head came clean off his shoulders and rolled away under a table. What fun! There was a **ROAR** of approval, but Gawain felt a little sad. If only the big guy had thought it through, he might have come up with a better game.

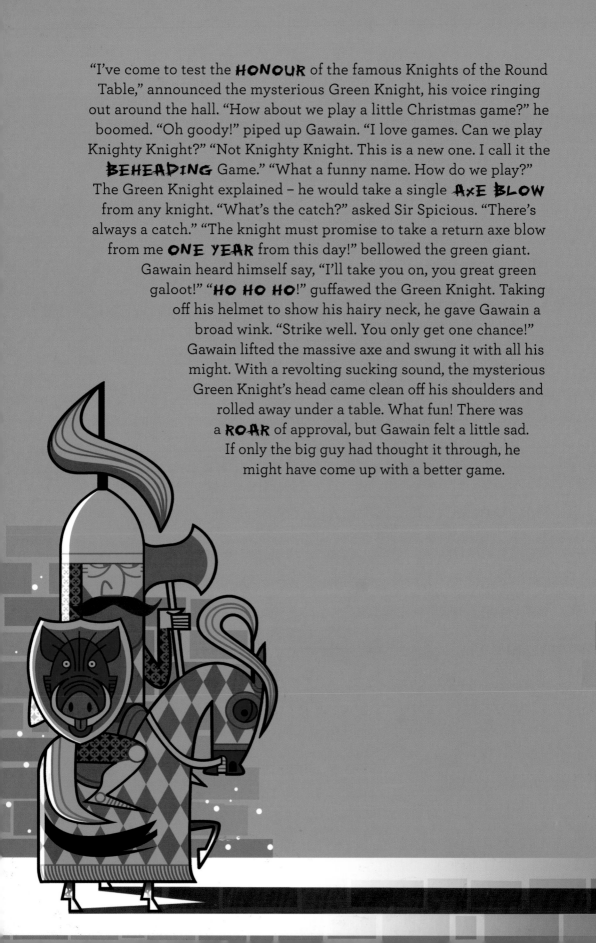

Just then the shouts died on the lips of the knights and ladies, for the Green Knight's body twitched. Standing up unsteadily, the strange giant swayed over to his **SEVERED** head and picked it up. The eyes fixed Gawain with a terrifying stare, and the lips called out clearly "See you next New Year at the **GREEN CHAPEL**, Sir Gawain. I'm already looking forward to it!" And with that, the mystery knight remounted, shouldered his splendid **AXE** and rode out.

The year passed quickly. Before Sir Gawain knew it, **WINTER** had rolled around. It was time to go in search of the Green Chapel. Tearful young ladies waved him off from Camelot. Gawain rode far and wide, but he could not find the Green Chapel. Finally, with just a few days left, he came to a castle. "You're in luck!" cried **BERTILAK**, the lord of the castle, after Gawain explained his mission. "The Green Chapel is close by. Why don't you rest up here till New Year?"

The next morning, after a light breakfast of fried quails' eggs, sea-otter sausages, and hog roast, Lord Bertilak went **HUNTING**. "Stay in the castle today," he said, as he left. "I'll give you my hunting spoils if you promise to give me everything you gain here." Baffled, Gawain agreed and spent the day with lovely Lady Bertilak. They played cards, read poetry, and got on brilliantly.

"I bet you kiss all the ladies in Arthur's court," teased Lady Bertilak. "Shame on you!" shot back Gawain. "I am a **CHIVALROUS** knight!" "A shivery knight?" laughed Lady Bertilak. "Well you'd better warm up by the fire!" And with that, she kissed him on the cheek. Soon after, Lord Bertilak returned. "Bah," he grumbled, throwing down a tortoise. "The deer were too swift. How did you get on, my friend?" True to his word, Gawain went over to his host and gave him what he had won that day – a **KISS**!

On the second morning, after a wholesome breakfast of duck pancakes, beef-shin fancies, and tortoise soup, Bertilak headed out hunting. Gawain stayed with the lady of the castle and had a fine old time. When the lord returned, he was in a foul mood. "The boar were too **CUNNING**!" he cursed. "A mere hedge-pig is all we won." Without a word, Sir Gawain surrendered his winnings – **TWO** kisses, this time!

On the third morning, over a healthy breakfast of turkey turnovers, pigeon sideshows, and hedge-pig fritters, Lord Bertilak's good spirits returned. He talked of the **BEASTS** he would bag. Gawain, however, was poor company that day. He knew that tomorrow he must face the Green Knight. "Don't worry, good Gawain," purred Lady Bertilak. "You must take my magic green **GIRDLE**! Wear it around your waist and it will keep you safe from any blade – especially a chunky axe wielded by a mysterious green giant!"

Shortly after, Lord Bertilak strode into the hall. "Success! We cornered a fox! Here, take it my honest guest!" In return, Sir Gawain planted **THREE** kisses on the lord's cheek – but remembering the Green Knight's fearsome axe, he kept the lady's magic green belt for himself. He would need all the **HELP** he could get...

On New Year's morning, after a hearty meal of badger bake, pheasant two ways, and a foxtail gumbo, Sir Gawain thanked his hosts. It was time to prove his mettle. Would he show himself to be a **TRUE** knight or would he back out at the last minute? Gawain slowly wrapped Lady Bertilak's magic girdle around his waist, strapped on every bit of armour he owned, and set out to meet his fate.

Before long, Gawain reached a snowy forest clearing. There was the Green Chapel – and there was the mysterious Green Knight, **SHARPENING** his enormous axe. "You came, Sir Gawain!" he shouted. Gawain dismounted, clanking.

"**HO HO HO**!" boomed the mysterious Green Knight. "With all that armour, it will be more 'Rust in Pieces' than 'Rest in Peace' when I've finished with you!" Gawain felt sick, but he knelt and took off his helmet. "I'm ready," he said quietly.

As the Green Knight swung his axe, Sir Gawain **FLINCHED**. "Ho ho! 'Tis no **BRAVE** knight we have here – 'tis a yellowbelly!" roared the Green Knight. "If you are a truly worthy Knight of the Round Table, then play the game properly!" Gawain **BLUSHED** and promised not to flinch next time. He heard the blade slicing through the air towards his neck but the Green Knight stayed his hand. "Are you monkeying with me?" challenged Gawain. "Just checking you weren't going to flinch again," mumbled the Green Knight, and swung again.

This time, the axe did break the skin, but Gawain's head stayed on his shoulders. King Arthur's knight leapt to his feet. "That's your turn over, you twisted green **MANIAC**!" he shouted. "Now prepare to **FIGHT** like a normal knight!" But instead of fighting, the Green Knight started laughing. Before long he was doubled up, crying with mirth. "I'm sorry, Gawain. I can't fool you any longer... I am Lord Bertilak! Those first two axe swings were for when you honoured our deal and returned the **KISSES** you got from my wife. But the last little **NICK** in your neck was for the lie you told me about the magic green girdle."

"Oh! I am a **WRETCHED** churl!" wailed Sir Gawain. "And unfit to call myself a Knight of the Round Table." "Don't be so hard on yourself!" replied the Green Knight—Lord Bertilak. "You told a tiny **WHITE LIE** to save your life, not because you are dishonourable. Now go home and face the judgment of your king."

Gawain returned miserably to Camelot, sure that he would be thrown out of the company of knights. Imagine his surprise when, as he finished his story, they all fell about **LAUGHING**. "From now on, we should all wear green girdles!" hooted King Arthur. And so they did. From that time onward, Sir Gawain's green girdle has been a symbol of honour.

BaBa YaGa

MARUSIA STOPPED AND SHUDDERED.
The path she was following led straight
into the dark forest. The trees leant in over
the path, and their branches CREAKED
and groaned. Her stepmother had
hoodwinked her into taking a basket of
goodies to "your BABA who lives in the
deep, dark woods".

All Marusia wanted to do was turn back, but she remembered what her **REAL** grandmother used to say: "Be good and kind to everyone, and nothing bad will happen." "OK." Marusia told herself. "Here goes!" She picked up her basket again and plunged deeper into the woods.

It was twilight by the time she came to Baba's cottage. There was no mistaking this was the place – **SPOOKY** didn't even come close! The lopsided wooden hut was in a terrible state. Was it swaying ever so slightly? Hang on a minute! What was it standing on? **CHICKEN LEGS**!

Reaching the door wasn't easy. A birch tree trailed its branches across the path. As Marusia pushed past, they wound around her ankles. But the girl just laughed, "Oh Birch, I think you're in need of a haircut!" Then she unwound a pretty **RIBBON** from her hair and tied back the branches with a neat bow.

A picket fence of ghastly **BONES** surrounded the property. When Marusia tried the stiff gate, it snapped back and **TRAPPED** her fingers. "What a squeaky greeting, Little Gate!" Marusia said, wagging her finger. She found some oil in her basket and poured it over the rusty hinges. "There you go! That should make you a bit happier."

On the garden path, Marusia met a **SCRAWNY** black cat. It yowled pitifully, and when she bent down to tickle it behind the ears, the cat **SCRATCHED** her. "Ouch!" she cried. "You poor thing! Are you hungry?" And out of her basket she pulled some ham. "There you go, Pusskins." Moving on, Marusia knocked bravely on the hut door.

The door swung open on its own. The place looked empty, but also a little cosier than it seemed from outside. There was an old **SAMOVAR*** boiling cheerfully on the stove. "Hello? Baba? It's me, 'Rusia..." called out Marusia, trying to keep the **WOBBLE** out of her voice.

"There you are, child!" Crouched on the ceiling like a huge **SPIDER** was her stepmother's mother. Marusia's "Baba" was none other than Baba Yaga – the **WITCH** of the North! "What took you so long?" complained the witch, her long, bony arms, and skinny legs cracking as she crawled down the wall. Marusia nearly screamed.

Baba Yaga sat down and began to file her iron teeth, **SHARPENING** each point. "Your stepmother doesn't like you very much, does she?" she said. "I think she **HATES** me," answered Marusia, honestly. "Good, good," the witch nodded. "I've got to collect some treats to go with supper. While I'm gone, I want you to clean the house and lay the table. Tonight we eat tender meat!" and the old witch **GNASHED** her teeth.

* A TALL, CURVY
RUSSIAN TEAPOT

Marusia swept, tidied, and tried not to cry. She laid the table for two. "You'll not be eating, child," said a voice. Looking down, she saw the **CAT** washing its paws. "Baba Yaga means to eat you tonight," said the cat, cool as that. "You must escape! First, though, take the **CLOTH** off the rack. When you hear the witch coming after you, throw it on the ground. Take that **COMB** from the dresser, too. When you hear her behind you, throw it on the ground. Now go!" The girl thanked the cat and fled into the dark forest.

Baba Yaga was busy setting the traps outside the hut. "Are you still hard at work, my dear?" she called out. "Yes, I'm working hard!" answered the cat from inside the house. When the witch finally came in and saw she had been **FOOLED**, she kicked the cat hard. "Why didn't you scratch the horrible little girl?" she screamed. The cat replied, "All these years I have caught mice for you and in return, all you've given me are kicks and **HARSH** words! The girl gave me tasty ham."

Cursing the cat, Baba Yaga stomped out and kicked the **GATE**.
"Stupid Gate, why didn't you stop the brat leaving?" The gate replied,
"All these years I have kept you safe from intruders and in return,
you've never given me a lick of paint or a drop of oil! The lovely girl
oiled my squeaky hinges."

Cursing the gate, Baba Yaga picked up a stick and hit the **BIRCH**.
"Useless tree, you are supposed to **WHIP** people who pass! I should chop
you down for being so lazy!" she roared. The tree replied, "All these years
I have been a good tree and in return you've never cared for me! I did not
want to spoil this pretty ribbon the little girl gave me." Baba Yaga was
FURIOUS. Storm clouds brewed above her head and lightning flashed.
She jumped into the big bowl she used for crushing bones, and
rode off in it to catch her escaped dinner.

Some way ahead, Marusia put her ear to the ground and heard the witch
coming. She threw down the cloth and instantly a wide **RIVER** sprang up.
On the opposite bank, Baba Yaga screeched to a halt. The witch got down
on her knees and began to drink the river. Marusia ran on.

Farther along, Marusia stopped to listen again. She heard a **RUMBLE** growing closer – the witch! Marusia pulled out the comb, kissed it, and threw it down. Instantly a great **FOREST** sprouted. On the other side, Baba Yaga clashed her teeth like cymbals and began to chew the gnarly, twisted trees. But the trunks were too knotted, too tough and too many. The Witch of the North wore her metal teeth down to the **GUMS** and had to go home hungry.

When Marusia returned safely, her stepmother dropped the chicken wings she was eating in surprise. Marusia smiled sweetly but the **WICKED STEPMOTHER** knew the game was up. By the time Marusia's father came home, she was long gone.

OSIRIS AND SET

FROM: COUNCIL OF THE GODS
DIVINE REALM, THE SKY

TO: ISIS, GODDESS OF MOTHERHOOD AND MAGIC
SOMEWHERE IN EGYPT

Re: CEASE AND DESIST
Dear Isis,
We are worried about the state of our beloved country Egypt. Things are getting worse and worse for the people, and we feel your **DIRTY** tricks campaign against King Set is to blame. May we remind you, even if he is a little bit weird, he is still the pharaoh. Please sort it out and/or leave him alone. Your caring mystical beings in the sky,

THE GROUP OF NINE

FROM: ISIS, GODDESS OF MOTHERHOOD AND MAGIC
A REED BANK, THE NILE RIVER

TO: COUNCIL OF THE GODS
DIVINE REALM, THE SKY

Umm... Gods,
You've got to be kidding me, right?!
Not only did Set trap his own brother, Osiris – the
RIGHTFUL king – in a specially made strongbox and
throw him into the Nile, but then he went and chopped
him into pieces! It took me years to track down all the
bits of my lovely hubbie and put him back together.
Even that wasn't enough to bring him back...

Osiris and I were all about love. I **WEEP** for him every year and the tears
I cry bring the floods that keep the soil fertile. So don't go lecturing me
about not caring for Egypt!

By the way, "weird" doesn't even come close where Set is concerned. He
drinks souls and smells funny. Aren't you gods supposed to know these
things? Didn't you know that he is the god of scorpions, wicked spirits,
anger, want, snakes, dirtiness, **CHAOS**, sandstorms, and plagues – how
can you possibly think he's a good choice for pharaoh?

Furthermore – to set you straight – I don't wish to be pharaoh.
I think the **RIGHTFUL RULER** of Egypt is Horus. As well as
being Osiris's and my son, he has a lovely beak.
Yours in sadness and hope,

ISIS

TO: COUNCIL OF THE GODS
DIVINE REALM, THE SKY

Dear Council,

Isis is nothing but a troublemaker. Egypt should be ruled by the strongest person. It's stupid to have it any other way, since the strong one always takes what he wants anyway. Since Osiris has **TRAGICALLY** departed (may he rest in "pieces", guffaw!), I am next in line – the strongest and the oldest. Horus is a weakling... and ugly too.

SET, RIGHTFUL KING OF EGYPT

FROM: COUNCIL OF THE GODS
DIVINE REALM, THE SKY

TO: ISIS & SET
EGYPT

Re: CHALLENGE FOR POSITION OF PHARAOH
To Whom It May Concern:
We have decided. Set is still the pharaoh, but if Horus wants to **CHALLENGE** him that's OK by us. May we suggest some water-based games on the Nile? We love watching river battles. Such fun! Regards,

THE GROUP OF NINE

TO: ANUBIS, PROTECTOR OF THE DEAD
THE UNDERWORLD

Anubis, you old dog!
How are things down there in the Underworld, my jackal-headed one?
Hope you're keeping a close eye on your Uncle Osiris – he's managed to
come back from the dead too many times for my liking. You may be the
best at making **MUMMIES**, but I swear that if you fail, it's you who'll
be wanting *your* mummy!

Keep swallowing souls, Wild Thing!

SET, YOUR CRUEL AND CRAZY KING

P.S.: I'll be coming after the Owl Boy v. soon.

TO: COUNCIL OF THE GODS,
DIVINE REALM, THE SKY

Oh Ye Gods,
No fair! Isis used her freaky magic to help Horus win. My armies were defeated when he chucked a terrifying, dazzling **SKY DISK** at us. If I find out that had something to do with you guys… you'll be sorry!

The boat race was fixed, too – it's definitely not my fault that my boat sank! OK, so maybe I made it out of stone. Whatever! Who can blame me for turning myself into a massive **HIPPO** and trying to sink Horus's fancy reed boat? How was I to know that he had a harpoon strong enough to turn me into a hippo-lollypop-amus?

SET, STILL PHARAOH AS FAR AS I'M CONCERNED

* *

TO: OSIRIS C/O ANUBIS, GOD OF THE UNDERWORLD

URGENT TELEGRAM

Things are a little "sticky" in Egypt. **STOP**. Who should be pharaoh? **STOP**. Thoth says it's only fair to pick Horus, but lots of us like Set. **STOP**. Dude is sick! **STOP**. We mean funny. **STOP**. What should we do? **STOP**. Yr advice IS always spot-on. **STOP**. The 9. **STOP**.

P.S. Dead sorry to hear about you being chopped up into 14 pieces. **STOP**.

TO: COUNCIL OF THE GODS
DIVINE REALM, THE SKY

Dear Group of Nine,
Set is in denial after the boat race – geddit? **IN DE NILE**. Oh forget it! Look, if it were up to me, Horus is the one. Nothing to do with him being my son. Honest.

Yours in love,
OSIRIS

P.S. It would be great if you could arrange for me to get out of here. Anubis is OK, but kinda **CREEPY** (he's in charge of weighing the hearts of the dead, but I guess you knew that already).

TO: EVERYONE IN EGYPT

Dear People of Egypt,
Re: A NEW PHARAOH

Rejoice, People of Egypt! Horus has defeated Set in the first great Battle of the Nile. In avenging the death of his father, he is to become the new pharaoh. All hail to **HORUS THE BRAVE**!

However, Set will not die. Horus the Good and Set the Evil will fight against each other for eternity (and that will be fun for us, too).

Our decision is final.

THE GROUP OF NINE

101

HOW ANANSI GOT HIS STORIES

FAR AWAY in a hot country, where the forests are thick, and dark, and the rivers are swift and strong, lived a **SPIDER** called Anansi. His web looked out over a village and at night the spider liked to watch the humans around their fires. But he had noticed something: the people were bored! The kids were naughty and the adults were cranky.

"What these people need are some stories to share," thought Anansi. But **NYAME**, the god of the sky, had all of the stories and he kept them locked in a box. "Tomorrow I will talk to Nyame," thought Anansi as he stretched out his eight legs, yawned, and went to sleep.

The next morning, Anansi spun a thread into the sky. He followed it until he came to the hall of the sky god. Nyame was powerful – tricking him would not be a good idea. Anansi was on his **BEST BEHAVIOUR**. He had even smartened himself up for the meeting, combing his bristles, and shining his eight eyes until they gleamed like black opals. He bowed low and said, "O great Nyame, I would like to have your box of stories to give to the people of the world. What is your price?" Nyame laughed so loud the heavens shook. "**HA HA HA! HO HO HO!**" said the sky god, wiping away a tear. "That's a good one, spiderling. Many rich kings and powerful sorceresses have tried to win my box of stories, but none have been able to pay the price. What makes you think that you can?"
"I can pay! I can pay!" insisted Anansi.

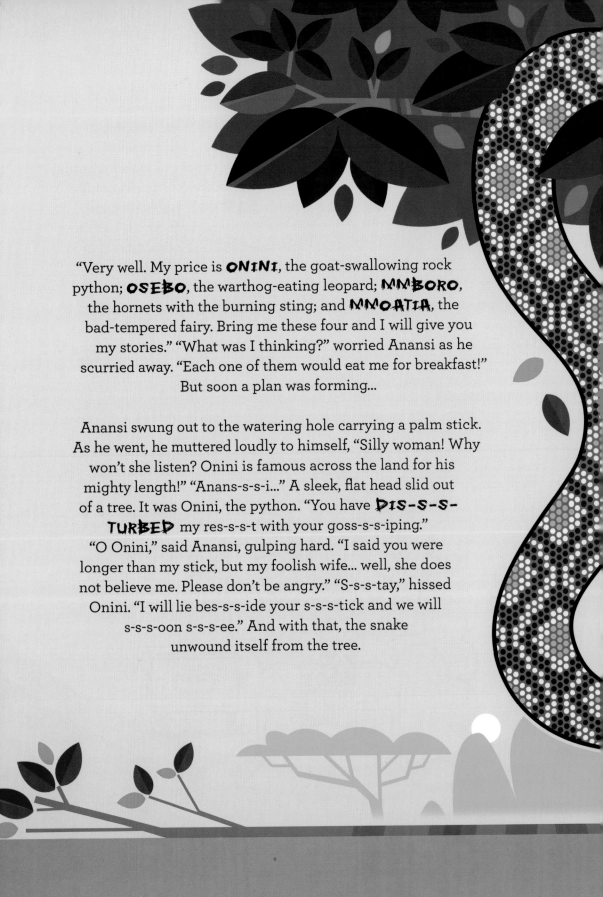

"Very well. My price is **ONINI**, the goat-swallowing rock python; **OSEBO**, the warthog-eating leopard; **MMBORO**, the hornets with the burning sting; and **MMOATIA**, the bad-tempered fairy. Bring me these four and I will give you my stories." "What was I thinking?" worried Anansi as he scurried away. "Each one of them would eat me for breakfast!" But soon a plan was forming...

Anansi swung out to the watering hole carrying a palm stick. As he went, he muttered loudly to himself, "Silly woman! Why won't she listen? Onini is famous across the land for his mighty length!" "Anans-s-s-i..." A sleek, flat head slid out of a tree. It was Onini, the python. "You have **DIS-S-S-TURBED** my res-s-s-t with your goss-s-s-iping." "O Onini," said Anansi, gulping hard. "I said you were longer than my stick, but my foolish wife... well, she does not believe me. Please don't be angry." "S-s-s-tay," hissed Onini. "I will lie bes-s-s-ide your s-s-s-tick and we will s-s-s-oon s-s-s-ee." And with that, the snake unwound itself from the tree.

"O Onini," said Anansi. "It is hard for you to straighten your whopping coils. Let me use my silk to hold you against the stick and get your true measure." The proud and **POMPOUS PYTHON** stretched out and was soon tied fast to Anansi's stick. "Ho ho ho," chuckled Anansi. "Now you will come with me to Nyame." The spider hauled the snake up to the heavens, but Nyame simply said: "I see what I see. There remains what remains."

Next, Anansi turned his attention to Osebo. Catching a leopard was going to take all his smarts. Working through the night, he dug a **DEEP HOLE** along the trail that Osebo took to the watering hole and camouflaged it with leaves and grass. The next morning, the forest was soon ringing to furious roars and **PITIFUL** caterwauls. Anansi came and peered over the lip of the hole.

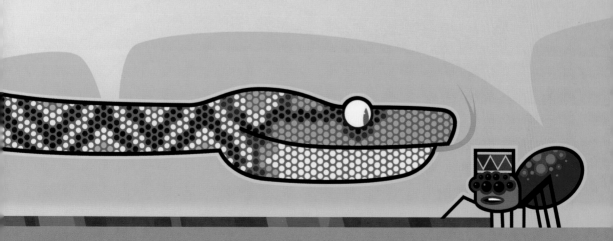

"Good morning, Mr Osebo! What are you doing in there? Are you resting, O great leopard?" "R-R-R-OAR! I'm not resting, I'm TRAPPED! Get me out!" snarled the leopard. "Oh no! If I let you out, you will gobble me up!" Anansi fretted. "My poor family – what will they do then?" "OK, OK. I promise not to eat you," said Osebo. "You are too heavy to climb on my web, but I will spin my strongest and stickiest thread for you," said Anansi.

The clever spider bent a young tree over the hole and held it with an anchor line. Then he spun a thick, sticky cord and told Osebo to attach it firmly to his tail. With the leopard stuck fast, Anansi cut the anchor line and the sapling whipped back, sending the **SILLY LEOPARD** sailing out of the hole with a giant yowl! Around and around the tree Osebo spun, until he was all trussed up! "Ho ho ho," chuckled Anansi. "Now you will come with me to Nyame." Anansi presented the silk-wrapped leopard to the sky god, but Nyame simply said: "I see what I see. There remains what remains."

Now, to a human being, the sting of a hornet is like a kiss from a red-hot needle dipped in itching power, but to a spider it is **DEATH**. Anansi would have to be very careful catching Mmboro. Anansi and Aso, his wife, hollowed out a gourd fruit and filled it with water. Dragging it to Mmboro's home, Anansi drenched himself and the nest in water. Maddened, Mmboro swarmed out to **PUNISH** whoever had done this. They came face to face with Anansi, who was holding a big banana leaf over his head. "Oh no!" cried Anansi. "The rains have come early! Run for your lives!"

"Whatz-z-z all thiz-z-z noiz-z-z-e?" buzzed the hornets. "A terrible storm is coming, my friends," said Anansi. "You can shelter in my gourd until it passes." "Thankz-z-z Ananz-z-z-i," said the **HUFFY HORNETS** and in they flew. With a twist of a stopper, the clever spider had a pot of bottled angriness. "Ho ho ho," chuckled Anansi. "Now you will come with me to Nyame." Anansi gave Mmboro to the sky god, but Nyame simply said: "I see what I see. There remains what remains."

Nyame's final demand was Mmoatia, a forest fairy who steals children. She's full of mischief, has a **TERRIBLE TEMPER**, and her feet point backwards so her tracks are hard to follow. Anansi had to come up with a very clever plan to foil her! First, he carved a wooden doll and then he covered it with gum-tree sap. It was fiddly, but the spider was used to working with sticky stuff. Meanwhile his wife Aso pounded yams and mixed them with eggs and oil to make **ANO**, a sweet paste that fairies can't resist. Then Anansi put his doll and the *ano* treats in a clearing where Mmoatia liked to dance. Before long, she came skipping by.

"My favourite! May I have some of your delicious *ano*?" Mmoatia asked the doll. Anansi had fixed a thread to the doll's head so he could make it nod. The fairy happily ate up all the yam paste and then put the bowl back on the floor. "Thank you very much," she said. But the doll didn't reply. This is where the fairy's bad temper kicked in. "I said **THANK YOU!**" yelled Mmoatia. Still the doll did not reply. "**THANK. YOU.**"

The little fairy flew into a rage. "I'll teach you to be so rude!" she screeched, and hit the doll. At once her hand was stuck fast to the **STICKY** gum. "Let go of me, you horrible thing!" squeaked Mmoatia and she slapped the doll with her other hand. The sticky gum held fast that hand, too. "You'll be sorry!" shrieked the crazy fairy and she attacked her gummy enemy again, kicking and biting until she was **STUCK FAST**. "Ho ho ho," chuckled Anansi. "Now you will come with me to Nyame." And so, Anansi brought the last gift to the house of the sky god.

Nyame beamed a dazzling smile, like the sun breaking through the clouds. "You have brought me everything I asked for, little one. Princes, chiefs, and rich villagers have failed but you have not." The heavens rang out to Nyame's voice: "**PRAISE** be to Kwaku Anansi! He has paid the price for the sky god's stories. From now on they will be called 'spider stories'!" And he gave his beautiful wooden box of stories to Anansi.

Later that evening, back on his comfy web, Anansi stretched out his hairy legs and cuddled up to Aso. Below them, the people **GATHERED** around their fires and told stories. They would have them to share forever.

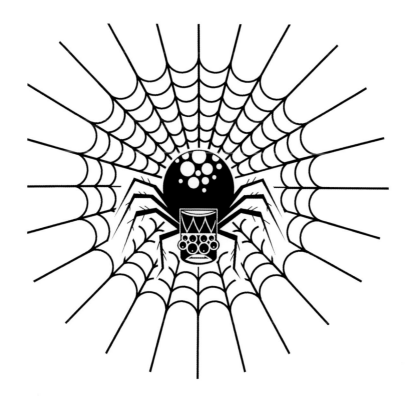

LOVELY LEOPARD ~~AND~~ DASTARDLY DOG

A LONG TIME AGO, before Anansi brought stories to the world, the dog and the leopard were **BEST FRIENDS**. They lived together in the wild bush. Each dawn they went out to hunt. When they returned to their cave, they **SHARED** what they had caught. If both came back empty-handed, they would lie close to each other and share their warmth, for an empty belly is easier to bear when you are with a friend.

Leopard leapt like she had **SPRINGS** in her paws and gave chase as if she was powered by rocket fuel. Her teeth and claws were like steak knives. In fact, it was fair to say that Leopard did all the hunting and Dog did all the eating.

"This is the life!" thought Dog, as he tucked into another of Leopard's suppers. The good eating was making Dog **LAZY** – on cold, wet mornings the pampered pooch hung back, unwilling to leave the cave. He was becoming **CUNNING**, afraid that his good friend might notice he wasn't doing his share of the work. One evening, Dog and Leopard sat talking over their plans. Leopard said that she was going to the village for a fine, **PLUMP** spotted goat. "That's funny, Leopard," said the mutt. "I'm hunting a spotted goat tonight too, but in a *different* village!" In the grey light before morning, Leopard slinked out of the cave and, taking care not to be seen, Dog sneaked after her. The cat found the animal pen and – **SPROING**! – with one leap she was over the wall!

BLAM! In a furry flash, the goat was down. The leopard swung her kill over the wall and was about to follow when Dog cried out in a crafty, disguised voice: "Wake up! Wake up! Leopard has killed a goat! Catch her!"

The villagers came running out of their huts, bashing saucepans – **CLANG**! – and throwing rocks and spears – **THUD**! **THUNK**! Leopard streaked out of there, running for her life. Dog snickered to himself, picked up the goat and trotted back to the cave. "Hello Leopard!" he said in his best surprised voice. "What happened to you?" A sorry-looking Leopard explained how she'd had to **SKEDADDLE** to save her spotty skin.

"Never mind. Thanks to lucky old me, we'll not go hungry tonight!" said Dog. And he heaved in the goat. "Let's chow!" Leopard set about making a fire and soon **DELICIOUS** smells were wafting out of the cave. Meanwhile, Dog found an excuse to go outside. The horrid hound took a stick and beat it on the ground – **WHACK**! **WHACK**! – and whined pitifully: "Oh please don't hurt me! It wasn't me! Leopard killed the goat! She's the thief!"

Leopard heard the row and cowered. "Oh dear," she thought. "The villagers must have followed me home and now they are beating Dog." And she rushed out to hide. Lying low in the grass, Dog watched her leave. Then he went back into the cave and ate the entire goat, bones and all – **BURP**!

Much later, Leopard crept back and found her so-called best buddy on his side: "**OUCH**! Don't touch me! Those villagers beat my bones so hard I hurt all over!" he moaned. "Poor Dog!" said Leopard, licking him tenderly. "Rest. **DON'T WORRY** about hunting."

Leopard set off for the village once again but the dastardly dog played the same trick. Good-natured Leopard was saddened by the change in her luck. Perhaps she was losing her skills? Why else did she keep getting caught in the act?

Leopard went to see **MZIMA**, the wise mole, who lives where the bush is deepest and the shade lasts all day. Although she is so blind she can hardly see the end of her nose, Mzima can see farther than most.

"Mzima," Leopard pleaded. "I used to be bold, swift, and strong, but now I am clumsy and take fright easily. Please help me find my luck again." "You know how to bring an animal down, but you must learn how to eat it. Do not look to your hunting skills, Leopard," advised Mzima. "Look to your **FRIENDS**."

Well, Leopard was bold, swift, and strong, but she was not bright. She went away with her pretty brow crinkled, **PUZZLING** over Mzima's mysterious words. She did not yet understand how it would bring back her luck, but she decided to keep an eye on her partner.

That night she told Dog of her plan to snag a fat brown goat. "No kidding!" cried the false friend. "Those brown goats are the sweetest!" Out in the cool dawn, Leopard did as she always did: **SPROING**! – over wall; **SWIPE**! – goat gone; **SLING**! – the kill sailing through the air. But this time, she circled around the village. There was Dog hiding in the long grass. "Wake up! Leopard has killed a goat! Catch her!" he called in his disguised voice.

"Hello Dog!" Leopard spoke sweetly, but her eyes **BURNED** like red coals. "Fancy seeing you here!" She smiled a slow smile that showed every one of her sharp, white teeth and raked her claws in the dirt.

The cowardly canine knew the game was up. He jumped up and ran as fast as his lily-livered legs would carry him, with Leopard close behind. Round and round the village they went, but Leopard was leaner and faster. To save his hide, the sorry hound dashed through a gap in the wall and into the village. **COWERING**, Dog came licking the feet of Man and begging mercy. Man took pity on him, tied him up and made him a pet.

Since then, Dog and Man have been friends, but Leopard has never forgiven Dog. Dog is always the first to sense when his **ENEMY** is near – his back bristles and he shivers with fear. Meanwhile, they say Leopard would rather eat a dog than a goat any day. This is how Dog and Leopard became enemies.

THE BLACKSMITH'S FIX

WALUKAGA HAD WORKED HARD all his life, perfecting the art of shaping metal. News of his smithing skills eventually reached the **KING**. Walukaga was summoned to the palace.

"If you are indeed the finest blacksmith ever," said the king, twirling his gold-handled fly whisk, "make me a **MAN**!" "But Great King –" began Walukaga. "No **BUTS**!" thundered the king. "I have been collecting metal for you to shape into a real man. I want him to eat and poop and talk – and clank when he walks!"

This was a **NO-WIN** situation. Building a living, breathing mechanical man was beyond even the famous blacksmith's great skills. If he tried to make a metal man, he would fail; if he didn't try, the king would beat him, throw him in prison, or worse...

Feeling hopeless, Walukaga walked deep into the **FOREST**. Just when he thought he was completely **LOST**, he heard crazy singing and cackling coming from a clearing – it was an old school friend who had disappeared years before.

"Greetings, Walu! The world's forgotten me, but I've not forgotten you," chuckled his bonkers buddy. "Come and eat with me." Over a meal, Walukaga told his crazy friend about the **FIX** he was in. "Listen to me," said the madman, chewing on a chicken bone, and then he told the blacksmith exactly how to save his skin.

It was late when Walukaga returned to the court. "Glorious King," he said. "Such a special item requires special materials. I need a **THOUSAND** loads of charcoal made from human hair, and a **HUNDRED** pots of salty tears to quench the metal." "No problem," said the king. "It will be easy for me, because I am the Great King!"

The king sent his servants across the land to clip, shave and pluck his people. But when all the hair was burned it produced only **ONE** load of charcoal. The king's subjects also blubbed and boo-hooed until they were all cried out, but their best efforts made only **TWO** pots of tears.

Walukaga was summoned back to the palace. "I am so, so sorry to disappoint you, Walukaga," said the king in a small voice. "You must be dying to show me what a great blacksmith you are, but I cannot provide what you need. My people cannot grow enough hair or cry enough tears, so I **RELEASE** you from your task." "Yahoo – I mean, **OH DEAR**, Great King," said Walukaga, trying to hold in a big sigh of relief. The blacksmith managed a respectful bow, then he turned and ran all the way home, whooping like a boy. People loved to tell the story of the **CLEVER** blacksmith, and of course Walukaga made sure his mad old friend never went hungry again.

MAUI OF ~~1000~~ 1001 TRICKS

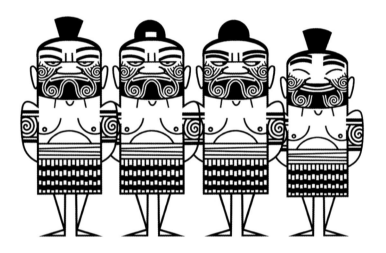

HI, MY NAME IS HINA. You won't have heard of me. I'm Maui's sister. Have you heard of Maui? You must have. **EVERYONE'S** heard of Maui! The dude who gave us fire and made the Sun shine longer? The trouble maker who fished our islands from the bottom of the ocean? Yeah, him. **MARVELLOUS MAUI.** Maui may have been a little fella, but when he was around there simply wasn't enough room for anyone else.

Maui was the ~~BABY~~ of the family. Then there's me, Hina – named after my mum, Hina – and my three older brothers – Maui, Maui, and Maui.

So that's four brothers I've got... all called Maui. Sheesh. If there were a prize for imagination, my parents would have got the wooden spoon! Little Maui had it tough, but he showed **PROMISE** right from the start. He was born early, and was weak and small. So what do you think my mum did? She tossed him into the sea! He didn't die, though, he **SURVIVED**. Maui was clever and he had the knack of staying alive.

Maybe Mum's cruelty shaped him – made him do the things he did. Maui was always trying to get back into her good books... y'know, trying to help make things easier for her. When Mum moaned that that there wasn't enough time in the day to weave her tapa cloth*, Maui decided to **HOLD BACK THE SUN** to make the day longer. Everyone knows that you can't stop the Sun, but try telling Maui that!

* A KIND OF CLOTH MADE IN THE PACIFIC ISLANDS
BY WEAVING WET STRIPS OF PAPERY TREE BARK

First Maui plaited some super-strong ropes from coconut shell fibres and used them to lasso the Sun but that was no good. The Sun just burned straight through them. Most people would have given up there and then, but not Maui.

He cut off my lovely, long **HAIR** while I was sleeping and made it into a noose. Then he crept to the eastern edge of the sea and caught the Sun by the throat just as it rose. Cor, that yellow **BALL OF FIRE** was angry – you could hear the yells for miles.

Eventually, Maui agreed to let the Sun go if he struck a bargain. The Sun agreed to travel more slowly across the sky for six months of the year, in return for being able to speed things up over the next six months. That's why we've got long days in the **SUMMER**, and short days in **WINTER**.

Mum was pleased, 'cos she could spend longer weaving. And everyone was all, "Maui, you're **AMAZING**!" and "Dude, you totally snagged the Sun!" Me? Well, what kind of jerk shaves off his sister's hair? They say the guy had a thousand tricks, but to me he was a walking practical joke!

Another time, my little bro tried to go with Maui, Maui, and Maui on a shark-fishing trip, but the older ones didn't want him along. They threw him off the boat into the water, chewing seaweed and **LAUGHING** at him. Boy, he was **MAD**. Little Maui went stamping all over the beach, kicking conches and shouting how he would catch the biggest fish – a kind they hadn't even heard of!

Off Maui paddled with his hook and line and – lo and behold! – he snared something **ENORMOUS**. It was way down deep and Maui had to really pull and heave. He could barely hold it, let alone land it. By now his brothers had gathered on the shore, watching in amazement. Maui asked them to wade out, jump into his canoe and paddle for all they were worth, while he struggled with the "fish". He also told them that they mustn't look back or it would break apart.

By now, it was pretty clear that this was no ordinary catch, but not to my dumb brothers. Maui had our **HAWAIIAN ISLANDS** on the end of his hook and was hauling them up from the bottom of the sea. Of course, my brothers did sneak a look and the islands broke up, just as Maui said they would – that's why they're like they are today. That guy was kinda freaky sometimes!

Maui got into so many scrapes, but eventually, he tried one trick too many. Mum had got sick and looked like she wouldn't live much longer. Maui said that she shouldn't worry – he'd go and get rid of **DEATH**, then we could all be together forever.

He'd been to the Underworld before, when he'd stolen fire from the **MUD HENS** that live there (that's a whole other story!), so he said it would be a cinch. But **NASTY** little songbirds woke up Hine-nui-te-pō (the great goddess of the night) before he was done and she squeezed the life out of my littlest bro. In the end, I guess, the joke was on him.

RAINBOW SERPENT AND THE WAWILAK SISTERS

DARKNESS LAY OVER THE LAND, just like it does when the stories are finished and it is time for sleep. The Sun, Moon, and stars slept and, without light, the world had no shape. Maybe things were there; maybe they weren't. Who could tell? The Eternal Ancestors slept too in the thick night, and there was no life and no death. This was the **DREAMTIME**, the place that exists along the Eternal Ancestors' songlines – not the Before, not the Time-to-Come, but the Great Always.

Then things stirred in the Dreamtime. In spaces that lie between a tick and a tock, the Eternal Ancestors began to sing the world into being. They danced around their dilly bags* in the darkness and brought the **LIGHT**, and their feet pressed the land into hollows and pushed it up into hills.

The Ancestors got busy **MAKING THINGS** that had never been seen before. They made trees and people and animals. Kangaroo got her pouch and Platypus got his bill. The songs brought to life Wombat and Wallaby, Kookaburra and Koala, Bandicoot, Possum and Potoroo.

* A TRADITIONAL AUSTRALIAN ABORIGINAL BAG,
WOVEN FROM PLANT FIBRES.

Into the Dreamtime came the Ngatyi – the **RAINBOW SERPENTS**. These massive and powerful Ancestors lived in deep, cool, water-filled caverns called *barambogies*, and they sparkled with many colours. There was a time when every watering hole was guarded by a rainbow serpent.

One evening the **WAWILAK SISTERS** stopped at a watering hole. They were tired after travelling across the land giving names to all the new things, and their babies were hungry.

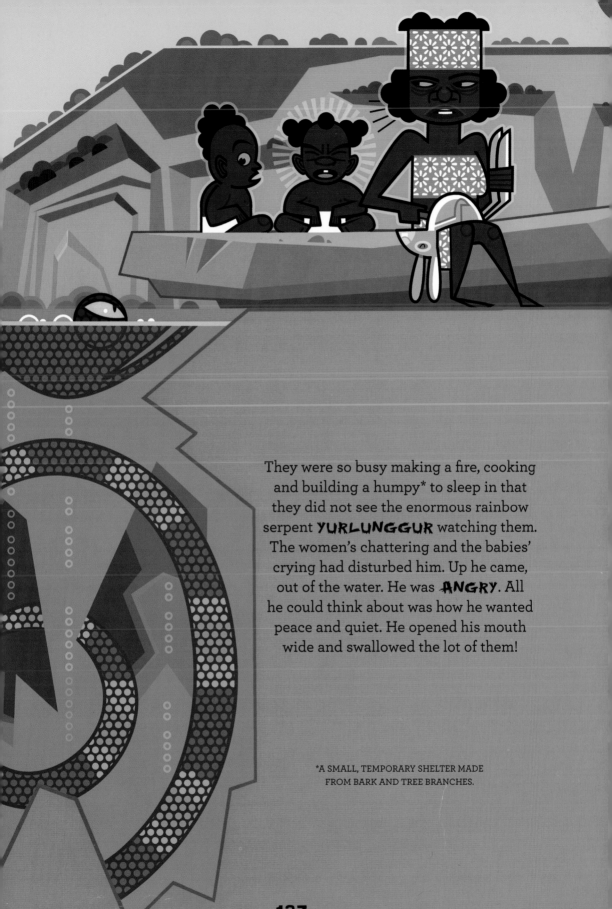

They were so busy making a fire, cooking and building a humpy* to sleep in that they did not see the enormous rainbow serpent **YURLUNGGUR** watching them. The women's chattering and the babies' crying had disturbed him. Up he came, out of the water. He was **ANGRY**. All he could think about was how he wanted peace and quiet. He opened his mouth wide and swallowed the lot of them!

*A SMALL, TEMPORARY SHELTER MADE FROM BARK AND TREE BRANCHES.

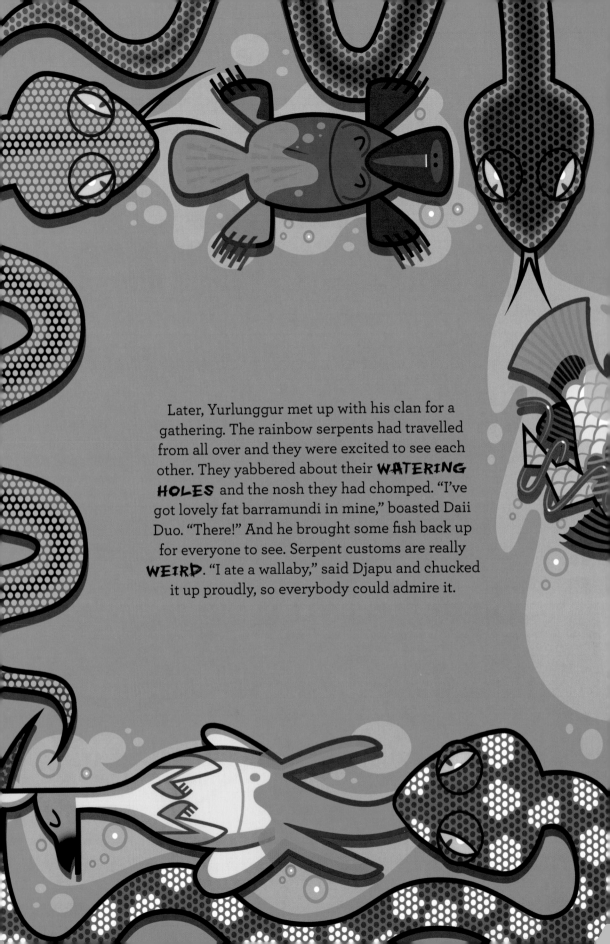

Later, Yurlunggur met up with his clan for a gathering. The rainbow serpents had travelled from all over and they were excited to see each other. They yabbered about their **WATERING HOLES** and the nosh they had chomped. "I've got lovely fat barramundi in mine," boasted Daii Duo. "There!" And he brought some fish back up for everyone to see. Serpent customs are really **WEIRD**. "I ate a wallaby," said Djapu and chucked it up proudly, so everybody could admire it.

Soon, every Ngatyi was bringing up his dinner. It was like a **PUKING** festival. The only one who didn't join in was Yurlunggur. "Come on, big brother," urged the snakes. "Show us what you've been eating." "Yurlunggur! Yurlunggur!" they chanted, but Yurlunggur wouldn't let his clansmen see. You see, he felt **ASHAMED** of what he'd eaten.

After a long time, Yurlunggur confessed in a small voice, "I ate two sisters and their babies, a small boy and girl." The Ngatyis were disgusted. "What terrible manners!" they hissed. "How could you eat your human guests?" It was a **DREADFUL** thing to do. Yurlunggur felt very sorry and his bright rainbow colours went pale. "I'm going to spew," he said, and he sicked up the Wawilak Sisters and their children. They lay there, covered from head to foot in **PYTHON JUICE** and dead, dead still.

The world fell quiet, waiting and hoping. Yurlunggur nudged the humans with his snout, but they did not move. Just then, a plump **HONEY ANT** came sauntering past. "Please sister," said the rainbow serpent. "I did a bad thing. Can you awaken these *wakus* and *yeppas* with your **STINGING BITE**?" The friendly honey ant gave each family member "ten of the best" with her sharp pincers. Now, the honey ant's bite is sharp and painful, and no human can possibly lie still when they are being bitten. As soon as they felt that ant, the family leapt to their feet with a **YELP**!

The stories of the Dreamtime are printed into the land. You can see the **TRACKS** that Yurlunggur made as he took the mothers and children back to their own country. You can see how he travelled through the heavens. When Yurlunggur got back to his *barambogie*, he slithered into his well, and entered its dark waters. And he **NEVER** ate another visitor for the rest of his life.

THUNDERBIRD AND THE WHALE

DEEP IN THE FORESTED, rainy mountains of the wild Pacific Northwest lives a mighty and magical creature called Thunderbird. The child of the North Wind and the South Wind, this **HUMUNGOUS** feathered fellow doesn't mess about. When he flies, his massive wings block out the sun, thunder rolls off them, and lightning shoots from his eyes. Whenever there's a storm, the weather-beaten people of the Northwest say to each other, "There goes that Thunderbird again." And then they remember the story of the **WHALE** to end all whales...

No one knew where the supersized whale came from, but it sure was **HUNGRY**. The monster gobbled up all the fish. It killed and ate all the other whales. Day after day the fishermen came home with empty nets – but what could they do? The whale had scoffed the lot. The hungry people called to the **GREAT SPIRITS** for help. Hearing their cries, the Thunderbird darkened the skies as he soared out of the mountains to the sea.

Thunderbird drove his **TERRIFYING TALONS** into the monster whale's back and tried to heave it out of the sea. But the whale was strong. SPLASH! It slapped the water with its tail and dived, plunging into the depths. Thunderbird was dragged under the waves by the mammoth marine mammal, but he held on.

The fight was a cruncher – this almighty collision was the most epic duel ever seen. They battled in the sea, sending huge waves crashing onto the shore. And – when the Thunderbird finally hoisted the whale ashore – they fought on dry land. Their struggle shook the ground as they **LAID WASTE** the earth, flattening trees and flinging them about by the roots. To this day, these areas remain treeless prairies. At last, Thunderbird defeated the whale: even though he was smaller in size, his **SPIRIT** was stronger. This is why the Thunderbird – known now as the Great Protector – sits on top of the totem pole.

HOW RAVEN STOLE THE SUN

RAVEN IS QUICK AND SHARP, and it is good to be nervous of him. Raven comes from beyond this world, and he keeps **SECRETS** that can both help and hurt people. He is great fun and will make you laugh and laugh, but watch out – he may be up to no good. Raven's favourite game is **DISTRACTING** people while leading them to do things that they do not want to do. Here is the story of one of his best tricks:

Back when **EARTH** was new, Raven was pure white. He had found humans trapped inside a clam shell on the beach. Lonely and wanting someone to play with, Raven set them free. But the world was **DARK**. An inky-cold blackness seeped into every crack and corner. It covered the eyes and clouded the shapes of things, making life hard and walking dangerous.

The people were cold and longed for the **LIGHT**, and Raven knew where to get it. An **OLD MAN** who lived in a house far upstream kept the **SUN** sealed in a box. Raven was a wild spirit and decided to steal the light. He perched outside the house on a branch, watching and waiting. When Old Man's daughter came out to collect water, Raven turned himself into a **PINE NEEDLE** and floated downstream. He timed it perfectly and glided into her water jar.

When the daughter drank water, Raven slipped inside her, where he turned into a **BABY**. A while later he was born as a little boy.

The Old Man doted on his grandson, giving him everything he wanted. The boy gurgled happily and chuckled with his grandfather's play, but what he liked most was the **BOX** on the high shelf. Light was the Old Man's most prized **TREASURE**. Sometimes he took the box down and opened it for the **JOY** of feeling the warm rays on his face. The little boy would cry and cry until his grandfather took the box down and once more filled the small house with light.

Old Man never allowed his grandson to hold the box until one day, when the child's pleading finally wore him down. This was the moment that Raven had been waiting for. Turning back into a **BIRD**, he took the Sun in his beak and flew up and out of the smoke hole. As he left, the smoke turned his feathers a deep charcoal **BLACK**.

Raven flew high and far – but higher still, **EAGLE** had spotted Raven. The king of the air came out of the sky like a thunderbolt and sunk his talons into Raven's back. Raven dropped the Sun and it crashed to the ground, spattering the **MOON AND STARS** across the heavens.

But the trickster managed to free himself from the Eagle's claws. Picking his **PRIZE** up again he raced as far as he could go – past the clouds and past the Moon to the very rim of the world. There, exhausted, Raven released the Sun. Light came into the world.

It spread from the **EAST**, lighting up the mountain tops, tinting them purple at first and then exploding into colours, while the snowy peaks shone **DAZZLING** white. Sunlight dipped into the valleys and fell on the trees and fields, making the birds sing with a joy for **LIFE**. Plants burst into flower and bees began their busy work. The people looked to the sky and were **HAPPY** at last.

GLOOSCAP MEETS HIS MATCH

GLORIOUS GLOOSCAP was the wildest warrior around. He had conquered cannibals and defeated devils. He'd brought giants low and tamed the **EVIL SPIRITS** of the night. In short, there wasn't anything that didn't bend to Glooscap's will in the end.
Or was there...?

One morning, Glooscap went for a dip in the river. The **AUTUMN** leaves clothed the scene in red, amber and gold, and ice was forming at the water's edge. Glooscap plunged in – a mighty warrior isn't afraid of a little cold! Surfacing and shaking his shaggy mane, he turned to face the sun feeling totally **EPIC**.

Just then, a woman came down to the river to fetch water. "Ho there! How goes it, Glooscap?" she asked, conversationally. "Pretty great, thanks," said Glooscap. "You know what I think? I think I must be the **BEST WARRIOR** there is." "Why do you say that?" asked the woman. "Well, it's obvious isn't it?" he said, taking in a deep, manly breath. "There's nothing the Gloo cannot do." The woman laughed. "Are you quite sure about that?" she quizzed. "Yup. One-hundred-and-ten percent sure!" "Ah," she twinkled. "I bet you can't overcome the one I serve!" "Who's that then?" asked Glooscap, irritably. "She is the **MIGHTY WASIS**," she replied. "I wouldn't tangle with her if I were you. She holds the past in one hand and the future in the other. And she gets whatever she wants."

"Take me to this stupendous bully," demanded Glooscap. "I'll show her a thing or two!" "She is right here," smiled the woman. She unwrapped her little baby from her papoose and plonked her on a rock. "This is the Wasis." "**GAH GAH**," gurgled the Wasis. "Ha! I'm not afraid of you!" said Glooscap. He raised his fists like a fearsome warrior. "Put 'em up and we'll soon see who's the stronger!" The Wasis sat and gurgled some more. Glooscap was annoyed. "I am the Lord of Men and Beasts. I command you to come here!" But the warrior's loud voice frightened the baby. The Wasis opened her pink mouth and **HOWLED**. She screamed and screamed. The sound would have frozen the blood of the most lion-hearted men.

"Great Spirits! Please stop that intolerable noise!" pleaded Glooscap. He thought his head would cave in. Glooscap tried his best warrior techniques. He danced his scary GHOST DANCE and sang songs that had made devils run back to the forests and mountains. But the more he stamped and fumed, the more the Wasis cried.

In the end, Glooscap had to admit defeat. The mother scooped up her baby and wrapped her back in her papoose. The Wasis stopped crying straight away. A big SMILE spread across her face. Not everyone has brought the Golden Age to Earth, but even the best warrior in the world must bend to the will of a baby.

RaBBiT STEALS THE FiRE

BRER RABBIT CONCENTRATED on making his headdress. It wasn't easy sticking on feathers with pine tar when you had big, fluffy paws, but the rabbit kept right on. Autumn was coming and the days were getting shorter. If Brer Rabbit's **PLAN** was to work, there wasn't much time left.

As the nights started to draw in, the animals of the **WOODS** came together in the evenings. They enjoyed being together as much for the shelter against the **DARK** as for the company. No one liked to talk about it, but they all knew that the days of cold and hunger were coming. Very soon winter would be at the door.

Life was different for the **WEASELS**. They had fire. On cold, dark nights the animals could see the lights twinkling merrily far off. They took turns imagining what it would be like to sit around a cosy, warming **BLAZE**, but they knew that getting fire from the Weasels was just a dream. The Weasels were a twitchy, bloodthirsty crew and Weasel Willage was surrounded by a high, thorny fence.

His headdress complete, Brer Rabbit decided it was time to put his plan into action. He strode right up to the gate of **WEASEL WILLAGE** and knocked loudly. "Hey Weasels! Great news! I've got a new dance to teach you!" he shouted. "Let me in!" "Get lost, pal!" came the none-too-welcoming reply.

"I heard that you're having a **JOLLY-UP** around the fire tonight," Rabbit persevered. "Yeah, we got us a clam-bake goin' most nights…" Rabbit continued, "I got a wicked new dance – you'll love it!" "No, no, Wabbit. We know your tricks! You sold us them 'magic gollygoober eggs' an' they weren't nothin' but river pebbles. Slitter broke 'is teeth on 'em. **SHOVE OFF**! We don't want nothin' to do with you!"

Rabbit waited a moment and then said slyly "I bet you're still dancing all those old numbers, like the shuffle and the slide. This one's a real **HEADBANGER** – it'll rock your world!" Now, if the wily Weasels had one weakness, it was music. They loved to dance – Rabbit was counting on it. There was much wheezing and whispering behind the fence, and then suddenly, the gate swung open. "OK Wabbit, you can come in – but no funny business!" hissed a Weasel with shifty eyes, who was chewing on a dead mouse. "You play it straight unless you want a bite on the schnoz!"

Rabbit strolled into Weasel Willage. He looked fabulous! His headdress of brightly coloured feathers flashed in the firelight. Tipped with pine pitch, each feather sparkled like a gem. The overall effect was **DAZZLING**! The Weasels led him to the dancing circle and stoked the fire until it blazed high into the night sky. "So go on then! Dance!"

Boy did Brer Rabbit **DANCE**! Around and around he went, kicking up the dust. Rabbit danced, bobbed and jigged. He swung his head low; he flung his head high. How the light of the fire bounced and played on the feathers of his merry headdress!

The Weasels were putty in the Master Dancer's hands. The beat was infectious, and the dance moves swift and clever. The fire popped and crackled, its colours changing, and they all joined in the dance. It was the **WILDEST** dance of all time. The Weasels were practically swooning as they tried to keep up with Rabbit's fancy footwork. Rabbit danced and danced. Faster and faster. Closer and closer to the fire, sweeping his headdress lower and lower...

WOOOF! The pine pitch on the feathers burst into a bright flame. Sparks flew and a fireball blew the Weasels back. "Watch out, Wabbit!" they shrieked. But Rabbit simply turned on his heels and ran, the flames streaking out behind.

One of the sharper Weasels screamed, "Wabbit's **STEALING** our fire!" Howling dreadful curses, the Weasels gave chase.

Rabbit ran and ran, but the Weasels were lean, tough, and tenacious. They called to the **THUNDERBIRDS** in the sky above to bring snow and hail and drenching rain, but the amazing headdress with its resin-coated feathers still burned brightly.

Rabbit was tiring now, so he called to **BRER SQUIRREL**. "Quick! Take the fire and run." Squirrel ran as fast as she could, but the heat from the fire made her tail curl up.

Squirrel was tiring, so she called to **BRER CROW**. "Quick! Take the fire and fly." Crow flew high, but the smoke from the fire turned his feathers black.

Crow was tiring, so he called to **BRER RACCOON**. "Quick! Take the fire and run." Raccoon raced away, but the ash left rings around her tail and face.

Raccoon was tiring, so she called to **BRER TURKEY**. "Quick! Take the fire and flee." Turkey was not a fast runner and the fire burned all the feathers off his head and neck. The fire was beginning to die.

"Set fire to my tail," said **BRER DEER** and off she went – so fast that the flames were fanned back alight. The fire burned off most of Deer's lovely long tail, leaving just a small stub behind. She heard the trees whispering to her, "Give us the fire. We will hide it. Give us the fire. We will hide it."

Deer was tiring, so she gave the fire to the **TREES** and they hid it in their wood.

The Weasels couldn't find it. "Let's leave this dingy place and get back to the Village," they hissed angrily.

Clever Brer Rabbit knew the secret of finding fire in the wood. He showed the other animals how to find it by rubbing the wood together. That winter, the animals had fire to warm their bones and brighten the nights. They sat around the **CHEERY BLAZE**, laughing and retelling the story of how Brer Rabbit stole the fire.

THE HERO TWINS

CHICHEN: WELCOME BACK to the Xibalba Death Dome, sports fans! AKA The Place of Fear! It's showdown time – the Hero Twins, Hunter and Jaguar Deer, challenge the Evil Lords of the Underworld in the final ball game of the series. It's winner takes all!

ITZA: That's right, Chichen. With skulls decorating the zi... zibal...

CHICHEN: It's Xibalba, Itza. You say it "Shee-bal-bah".

ITZA: Well, it's certainly a beautiful ball court – the *what-d'ya-call-it* – Death Dome, where the penalty for losing a ball game is cake.

CHICHEN: Don't you mean death?

ITZA: Oh yes. Death.

CHICHEN: The stakes are higher than ever tonight. Having lost all their matches in the lead-up, this is a must-win for the Twins. There'll be plenty of talent on show...

ITZA: And sneaky tricks!

PLAYERS
(LEFT TO RIGHT)

HERO TWINS

PUS MAKER
CAPTAIN: ONE DEATH
FLYING SCAB
VICE CAPT.: SEVEN DEATHS
BILE-MAKER
BLOODY TEETH
BLOODY CLAWS
PACKSTRAP
SKULL
BONE

CHICHEN: With any luck. As you know, the aim of the Mayan game of *Pitz* is to put the ball through the stone hoop, with as much dirty play as possible...

ITZA: And blood?

CHICHEN: Yes. Most probably lots of blood...

ITZA: And death?

CHICHEN: Yes, if we're lucky, some deaths.

ITZA: You can't beat a good noble death.

CHICHEN: Stay with us and you won't miss a second of the action. Coming up we have a courtside exclusive with the Hero Twins. But first a message from Skull-Owl, our sponsors:

GOT A MESSAGE TO DELIVER? SEND IT BY SKULL-OWL™. A MESSENGER FROM THE LAND OF THE DEAD IS GUARANTEED TO GET YOUR MESSAGE ACROSS!

CHICHEN: We've got a Skull-Owl right here... keeping an eagle eye on us – I mean "owl" eye. There's a good Skull-y...

ITZA: Brrr. It gives me the creeps!

CHICHEN: The noise in this ball court is deafening – as far as I can see no one is supporting the Twins.

ITZA: No one dares support them! After all, the Place of Fear is the home ball court of the Lords of the Death.

CHICHEN: They are the firm favourites in this grudge match. There's history here, as you know. So, as the teams file out on to the court, let's cross over to Tikal in the commentary box.

ITZA: ...Nice Skull-Owl... Ouch!

TIKAL: Yes, you're right on the cocoa beans there, Chichen. It's great to see the Dark Lords in action again. They humiliated the Hero Twins' father and uncle – and then chopped off their heads! Hopefully we'll get more of that meaty stuff tonight!

Here come One Death, the captain, and Seven Deaths, his vice captain. Wow! Talk about dressed to kill! Pus-Maker and Bile-Maker are out next – demons who sicken people; then Skull and Bone who turn bodies into skeletons; Bloody Teeth and Bloody Claws, the mayhem makers; and finally Flying Scab and Packstrap. Facing them are the Hero Twins: Hunahpu – "Hunter" – and Xbalanque – "Jaguar Deer".

But what's this? A scuffle's broken out before the game has even started! The Twins want to play with *their* ball. They claim Xibalba's ball is a cheat. Well, it looks like an ordinary skull to me... Anyway, the Underworlders say that it's their home turf, so they get to choose the ball.

We're underway. Oof! Skull and Bone try to bodyslam Jaguar Deer, but he is too fast! This is what we came to see – it's already a game of life and death out there. Ah, now that *is* delightful – the ball has sprouted razor-sharp blades. And I was worried that the Evil Lords would play fair!

Well, this is highly unusual. Hunter and Jaguar Deer are walking off.

I can't quite make out what Hunter's saying but he sounds really mad. Looks like they're leaving. But what's this? If I'm not mistaken, One Death is asking them to stay. He has agreed to play with the Twins' ball instead. Wow! The all-powerful Lords have backed down – I don't believe it and neither do the crowd! We're going to a commercial break now.

TIKAL: I'm courtside with the Hero Twins. Tell me, Hunter,

when your grandmother was trying to make honest farmers out of you, did you ever suspect you'd end up here?

HUNTER: Totally, dude. This is our destiny!

TIKAL: Talk us through your last match. How did you get through it in one piece?

HUNTER: One piece? I didn't, man!

JAGUAR DEER: The Lords put us into the House of Bats the night before that game. Those flesh-eating vampires would have had us, but we hid inside our blowpipes.

TIKAL: Very cunning.

JAGUAR DEER: Hunter peeped out to see if the sun was up yet, and one of those monsters bit off his head. When we got to the ball court, the Lords were using it as the ball. There was no way I could beat the whole team single-handed so I made Hunter a new head out of a pumpkin.

TIKAL: I bet the folk of Xibalba thought they'd won?
JAGUAR DEER: Yeah, man. But halfway through,
I managed to swap the pumpkin for the real head
and – bingo! – Hunter was back in the game!
TIKAL: When the pumpkin smashed on the hoop
and showered the Lords with gooey seeds... I think that
was the best thing I've ever seen!

TIKAL: Well, the game has restarted... A nasty tackle by Flying Scab...
but Hunter dances around him and the Scab falls flat on his face. The
Twins have taken it to another level tonight – these flagrant fouls are
very "dis-Mayan"! Go Twins! The next hoop will win the game for sure.

Slamdunk! It goes to the Hero Twins! With a name
like that how could they fail? It's utter "Twinsanity" down
here – back to you in the studio, Chichen and Itza.

CHICHEN: We have witnessed something incredible tonight!
A pair of hellraisers from a small Mayan village have defeated
death – truly "a-Mayan–zing"!
ITZA: These guys deserve to be as famous as the
Sun and Moon. Thanks for watching and, as we say
in Mayan, *jach dyos b'o'otik* – goodnight!

THE ARMADILLO WHO WANTED TO SING

IN THE FORESTS OF BOLIVIA, there lived a scratchy armadillo. Each day he went snuffling through the leaves picking out crunchy insect treats. Now, everyone knows that armadillos are nothing more than a turtle stuck on top of a rabbit – and **TASTY** too, with salt, pepper, and pineapple – but this 'dillo was different.

One day, while digging for grubs, the armadillo heard a sound. He raised his piggy snout and pricked a pointed ear to listen. What **SWEET MUSIC** – it was beautiful! The little armoured one went over to have a look.

PAD, PAD, PAD

In a splash of sunlight on the forest floor, a band of **CRICKETS** had struck up a tune. **MY**, they were good! The larger ones sawed away, thrumming out a toe-tapping bassline with their back legs, while the young 'uns chirruped

166

and riffed over the top. The armadillo
stood listening, delighted to his very core.
"Oh," breathed the 'dillo. "I would **LOVE** to
be able to sing!"

Now, armadillos do have some surprising talents.
When they're frightened, for example, they can jump
straight into the air. But there's one talent they *don't*
possess, and that's **SINGING**.

The armadillo plucked up his courage. "Say, crickets," he said.
"Could you teach me how to sing like you?" "Snicker snickety snicker!"
whizzed the crickets. "You look like a **HAIRY** piece of bacon rind!
You've got to be pulling our legs. Armadillos can't sing!" Armadillo
did not speak cricket, but it didn't matter. He was happy to just listen
to their **MUSICAL** voices.

He decided to give this singing thing a whirl... "**WHURGH WHURGH
WOAH-OH-OH**!" What a racket! It sounded like a bag of gravel falling
downstairs. The crickets gasped and **GIGGLED**. They rolled on their
backs with their legs in the air. The poor 'dillo sighed and shambled off.

That night, curled up inside his cosy burrow, he dreamed he could sing –
REALLY sing, making music with his whole body. And when he woke he
heard a new sound. It was **WONDERFUL**. He just had to check it out.

PLOD, PLOD, PLOD

A chorus of **FROGS** had assembled at the lake to sing in the moonlight.
Oh, what marvellous tunes they had – they bounced the tune back and
forth across the water until the whole pond **THROBBED** to their
rich tones. "Oh my," marvelled the 'dillo. "How I **WISH** I could sing!"

Now, armadillos do have some surprising talents. They can walk
underwater, for example. But there's one talent they really *don't* possess,
and that's **SINGING**. "Excuse me, frogs," piped the music-lover. "Could
you teach me how to sing like you?" "Ho-de-croakedy-ho!" gurgled the
frogs. "You **SILLY** turtle-rabbit! Armadillos can't sing!" Armadillo did
not speak frog, but it didn't matter. Even when they were laughing at him
it sounded so **GOOD**.

Feeling inspired, he tried to join in with their song...
"**WUG WUG WUGGA WOO**!" What a racket! It sounded like a box
of nails rattling in a steel tin. The frogs whooped and **WARBLED** with
mirth. Armadillo was sure he had got all the right notes, but they seemed
to come out in the wrong order. He sighed and wandered off.

Not long after, the armoured insect-eater was busy going to work on a
nest of fire ants when a flock of **SONGBIRDS** settled in the branches
above him. Their singing was a symphony. They trilled and twittered,
darting from high notes to low notes, and never singing the same thing
twice. It was **BEAUTIFUL**. Armadillo was in raptures.
"I **SO** wish I could sing," said the armadillo.

Then, growing in confidence, he added his own melody line to the mix...
"**WIH WIH WIZZ-UH**!" What a racket! The sound – like a cat being
sat on by an elephant – scared the birds and they **FLEW AWAY**,
taking their music with them. Armadillo felt sad.

He decided to visit the **WISE WOMAN** who lived in the woods.
All the animals went to her with their problems and maybe she
would help him to sing. Armadillos are not quick and it took him
many days of slow trundling to reach her house. As his long claws
came across the threshold –

CLICK, CLICK, CLICK

– the old lady stopped what she was doing and looked up.

"Hello there, Mr Armadillo," she welcomed him. "What can I do for you?"
"Oh great Wise One," he said. "There is **NOTHING** I want more in the
world than to sing." The witch was amused, but did not let it show – she
knew that even armadillos have feelings. She got low to the ground and
looked the mini-tank in the eye. "I can make you sing, little armadillo,"
she said, carefully choosing her words. "But the **PRICE** you would have
to pay is too high." "I would do **ANYTHING** to sing like the crickets,
and the frogs, and the birds," insisted the armadillo.

The wise woman had tears in her eyes, for this was truly a fine beast,
but her course was set. She killed the armadillo and carefully crafted
a **CHARANGO*** with his hairy shell. When the wise woman played
the musical instrument it made a beautiful sound. Everyone who heard
it exclaimed, "My goodness, the armadillo has learned to sing!"
People came from far and wide to hear the armadillo's music.

So never listen to what others say you can and can't do – after all,
what do they know? But **REMEMBER**, sometimes you might get
what you want, but not in the way that you expected!

* A MUSICAL INSTRUMENT WITH 10 STRINGS AND A BODY
MADE FROM AN ARMADILLO'S SHELL, FOUND IN THE
ANDEAN REGIONS OF SOUTH AMERICA

SACI PERERÊ

YOU MAY THINK that you know about Saci Pererê. You've heard that he is a **DEVIL**. But this is just what you've *heard* about him. Would you be brave enough to get to *know* Saci Pererê?

Meet Remédia Risolene Ruffles de la Rosa Mistica. With a name like that, it's no wonder they call her **FORMIGA**! It's Portuguese for "Little Ant". See, she might not have been built on a grand scale, but she was a **TOUGH** critter!

"Take this plate of beans up to Tio Pepé, little one," called Formiga's mother from the kitchen. "Mamãe, I'm **BUSY**!" Formiga replied. She was busy conducting a scientific experiment into how long it would take a sweet to dissolve in her mouth. It was tricky and required more than one test. Besides, Tio Pepé lived *waaaay* at the top of the steep hill.

"Remédia Risolene!" reprimanded her mother. When Mum used her proper name, she meant business. Formiga puffed up the flight of concrete steps to Tio Pepé's.

Nobody had much around here, but they **SHARED** what they had. This is what made the *communidade* strong – people looked out for each other.

Tio Pepé was a funny, **SUPERSTITIOUS** old gent. "Always stick to the paths," he'd say. "Otherwise the **COBRA-GRANDE*** might get you, or the **LOBISOMEM****." Tio Pepé's home was bursting at the seams. Hanging from the ceilings were tinkling mobiles made from old CDs, bottle tops, and metal bits and treasures from the tip.

* A HUGE, MYTHICAL SERPENT THAT LURKS IN THE AMAZON RIVER BY DAY AND COMES OUT AT NIGHT.

** A MYTHICAL, BLOOD-SUCKING MONKEY MONSTER WITH AN EVIL FACE AND BALD HEAD.

"What's in here, Uncle?" Formiga asked. She'd spotted a sealed **BOTTLE** tucked away on a shelf. "*Não toque* – don't touch!" Tio Pepé said sharply. "That's Saci Pererê," he went on, more gently. "Who's Saci Pererê?" questioned Formiga. "Who is Saci Pererê?!" spluttered the old gent. "What do they teach you kids nowadays? Saci Pererê is a little devil. He wears a red cap and his eyes glow red when he's angry. He's only got one leg, and he travels around in a dust devil – a spinning column of dust. He puffs on a pipe and has smoking holes in his hand." "He sounds nasty!" "Well, yes – he's definitely a **TROUBLEMAKER**…"

Tio Pepé paused, scratching his head. "Have you ever put something down somewhere, only to find it's gone a moment later?" "All the time," admitted Formiga. "**SACI PERERÊ** moved it!" announced the old man. "And have you ever done a poo, and found there's no loo paper?" Formiga wrinkled her nose. "Saci Pererê?" she guessed.

Tio Pepé was on a roll. "Flies in the soup. Burnt cooking. Tangled kite lines. Power cuts when your favourite *futebol* team are in the final. All Saci Pererê's fault! I was working on a construction site the first time I saw him. It was a **DISASTER** – the ladders broke, the concrete wouldn't set, and all the electrics kept blowing up."

Tio Pepé went on: "They say if you leave Saci Pererê a little offering of *cachaça** or tobacco, then he won't bother you, but I decided not to take any chances. I caught him in a **MAGIC** sieve and put him in this special bottle. That fixed him, for sure!"

Formiga loved Tio Pepé's stories but she never believed a word of them, of course. On the way home, though, she suddenly smelled a whiff of tobacco. "Yuk!" she coughed. Then Formiga thought she heard a **BOOM BOOM BOOM** behind her. She glanced back, but there was no one. The stairs were deserted. "My mind's playing tricks," she thought. "It's Tio Pepé's stories making me imagine things." Even so, when a dry wind picked up, Formiga quickened her step.

The week that followed was a **NIGHTMARE**. It rained non-stop and everyone grumbled. Dogs howled, and no one got a wink of sleep. Hens wouldn't lay. The milk was sour in the morning. Toys broke. Old folk complained of toothache, babies wailed, people worked late, and parents were cranky.

"Saci Pererê's behind all of this," realised Formiga. She marched off to see Tio Pepé. The old man's face told her all she needed to know. "Saci Pererê escaped. After you left, I felt an urge to look at that bottle," he said. "But I dropped it and it **SMASHED**. Oh, he's a clever one alright." "Don't worry Uncle," said Formiga, "I'll sort out that rascal."

* A POPULAR ALCOHOLIC
DRINK IN BRAZIL MADE FROM
FERMENTED SUGARCANE.

The brave girl set off, and before long she heard a **BOOM BOOM BOOM** behind her. A strong wind brought the smell of pipe tobacco. "Ha! I know that's you, Saci Pererê," said Formiga. "Where are you?" "RIGHT HERE!" a voice boomed in her ear. Formiga spun around, but there was no one there. "Now I'm over here!" taunted the voice. Formiga wheeled around and a pair of **GLOWING EYES** rushed at her.

"Why you meddlesome mayhem-maker..." Formiga began angrily, but then she remembered something Tio Pepé had said. Quickly knotting a rope, she dropped it on the path.

Soon the **LITTLE DEVIL** had stopped bugging her and was sat cross-legged trying to untie it, puffing furiously on his pipe – the boy couldn't resist a puzzle!

"Saci Pererê," said Little Ant. "Why are you such a **PAIN** to everyone?" The little devil's eyes flashed red. "Everybody hates me," he sulked. "They say nasty things!" "That's just words – you *do* annoying stuff," replied the girl. Saci Pererê's bottom lip quivered. "Listen," Formiga said brightly, before he could start to cry. "I bet you're really lots of fun to hang out with. Why don't you come with me to the dance on Friday?"

And so, Saci Pererê went to the dance. He may have had only one leg, but boy could he move. As the crowd whooped and cheered, a grin spread across Saci Pererê's face. This felt **GOOD**. Maybe he would turn over a new leaf and stop plaguing people. Formiga may have been mini, but she had a **MAXI** impact on those around her!

MONKEY BUSINESS

IT'S TRUE WHAT THEY SAY: "Things are not what they seem; nor are they otherwise." And that's never more true than in the case of Sun Wukong, the **MONKEY** who would be king. They say this monkey never had a mother monkey. They say he came out of a **STONE** that fell from the sky. Whatever the story, they all agree that Sun Wukong was unlike any other primate.

But we're getting ahead of ourselves. At first he was just **STONE MONKEY**, and a strange little fella he was, too. The other monkeys on Flower-Fruit Mountain got on with their own monkey business – collecting fruit and nuts, hanging out with their troop and squabbling amongst themselves. But Stone Monkey was different. He had a steely desire to make something of himself. Unlike the rest of them, he figured there was more to life.

On hot days, the monkeys chilled out by a beautiful pool that was fed by a roaring **WATERFALL**. The primates were afraid of its power and told each other it was sacred, and that no monkey could pass through it. "What a load of baloney!" scoffed Stone Monkey, and he took a mighty **LEAP** through the cascade.

"Well, I'll be a monkey's uncle," breathed Stone Monkey behind the falls. He'd discovered a **HIDDEN CAVE** and a steel bridge leading to wonderful halls carved out of the mountain. What a stroke of luck! He led the monkeys into their new home and they crowned him the Great King of a Thousand Years. Taking the throne, Stone Monkey banned the word "stone". From now on, he declared, he should be known as **HANDSOME MONKEY KING**.

That should have been enough for any primate. But soon Monkey was itching for **ADVENTURE**. Leaving everything behind, he set off. He travelled far and wide. He saw how others lived and he learned a great deal. Eventually, though, he tired of the world, so he went in search of **XIAN**, the immortal genie who lives between Heaven and Earth.

"Who are you?" asked Xian when Monkey finally came knocking. "You can call me Handsome." Xian ignored that! "What do you wish for?" he asked. "Well, I want you to train me up. I need some mad skills if I'm going to **RULE** over everything," said Monkey. Xian wasn't interested in Monkey's quest to master the universe. "Strip yourself of your **PRIDE** and ambition. These things won't do you any good. Now go on your way," said the genie.

But when he heard that Monkey was born from a magic stone, he changed his mind. Perhaps this proud primate was different after all. Xian took Monkey in and gave him a new name – **SUN WUKONG**, which means, Monkey Awakened to Emptiness.

Sun Wukong was a good apprentice at first. He learned how to change his body into 72 different shapes and he mastered the art of **CLOUD-HOPPING**, flying 35,000 miles in a single bound. But then he began to get fed up. "When will I finish my training?" he moaned. "When you quit monkeying around," replied Xian gruffly. "You stop being a student and become a great master when you realize that you don't exist."

Sun Wukong decided that he'd had enough of hard work. Keen to try out his awesome powers, he flew back to Flower-Fruit Mountain. On his way there, he broke into the Dragon King's palace and stole his **MAGICAL STAFF**. Just to test it out, Sun Wukong splatted the Milky Way out flat with one stroke. Not bad!

The **HEAVENLY SPIRITS** noticed the mayhem the monkey was causing. It was time to teach him a lesson. They locked him up in Hell, but Wukong had no intention of rotting away in the dark. He overpowered his guards and escaped. On the way out he spotted the Book of the Dead and tore out his name. Sun Wukong finally had what all that hard training had failed to give him – **IMMORTALITY**!

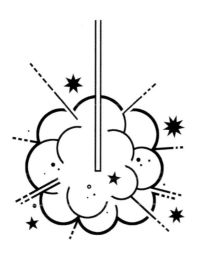

PRIMATE DAILY

THE RISE AND RISE OF HANDSOME MONKEY KING

Our most humble, benevolent, and gracious Great King of a Thousand Years, Sun Wukong, has a new job in Heaven. Starting on Monday, Sun Wukong takes the position of **MINISTER OF PEACE AND QUIET**, created especially for him.

The Council of Heaven released a statement yesterday saying they were **THRILLED** to welcome a new member to the team, and insisting that the move had "nothing whatsoever to do with keeping that pesky monkey quiet".

Peace returned to Heaven and Earth, and for a time Sun Wukong was happy. If he had one tiny niggle, it was that there wasn't all that much for the Minister of Peace and Quiet to do. One day he came across a garden surrounded by a tall wall and a locked gate. Bounding up onto the wall, he called to the girls inside who were picking peaches from the trees: "Hey! Chuck us a peach!" The girls giggled. "Not on your nelly! These are **PEACHES OF IMMORTALITY** and they're for the party." "What party? I haven't been invited to a party!" said Monkey, very affronted. "Why would you expect an invite," they tittered. "You're nothing but a stableboy!"

WHHHHAAAAATTTT?! Monkey's blood boiled. It was like that, was it? They'd tricked him! Well, if he really was nothing but a stableboy, there was nothing to stop him turning the Horses of Heaven loose! Full of **RAGE**, Monkey made the horses stampede, smashed up Heaven and ruined the party.

Monkey was dragged in front of the Lord of Heaven, the **JADE EMPEROR**. "Sun Wukong, you are the loudest, rudest, busiest, noisiest, most annoying monkey ever born! What do you have to say for yourself?" "I don't give a monkeys what you think of me!" sneered Monkey. As **PUNISHMENT**, the emperor had him put in a cauldron over a fire. It was so lovely not to have Monkey around, they forgot all about him. Forty-nine days later they remembered. Of course he was not dead – Sun Wukong was immortal. But instead of eyes he now had burning **HOT COALS**, and his fury was demonic.

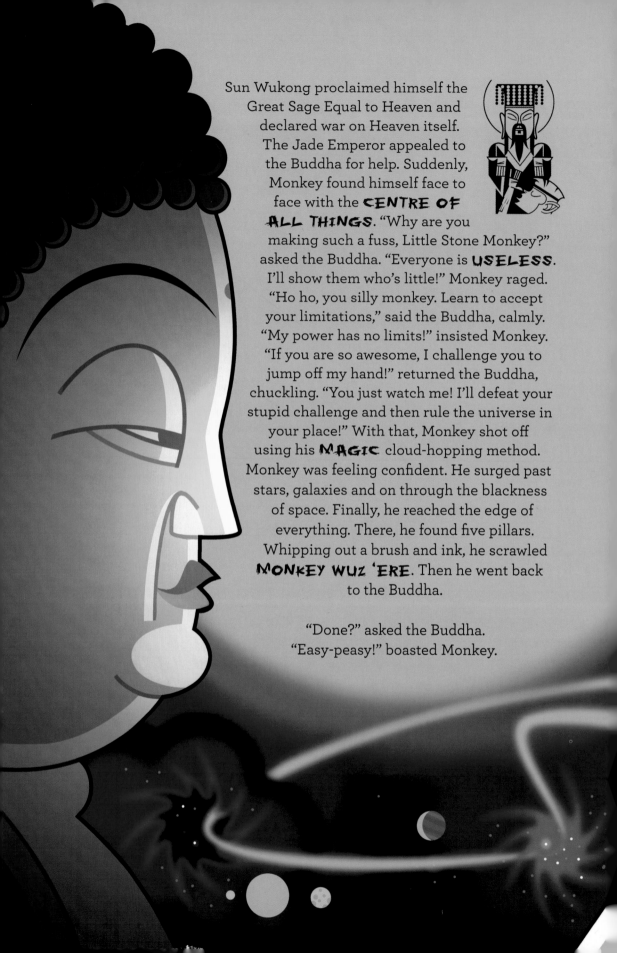

Sun Wukong proclaimed himself the Great Sage Equal to Heaven and declared war on Heaven itself. The Jade Emperor appealed to the Buddha for help. Suddenly, Monkey found himself face to face with the **CENTRE OF ALL THINGS**. "Why are you making such a fuss, Little Stone Monkey?" asked the Buddha. "Everyone is **USELESS**. I'll show them who's little!" Monkey raged. "Ho ho, you silly monkey. Learn to accept your limitations," said the Buddha, calmly. "My power has no limits!" insisted Monkey. "If you are so awesome, I challenge you to jump off my hand!" returned the Buddha, chuckling. "You just watch me! I'll defeat your stupid challenge and then rule the universe in your place!" With that, Monkey shot off using his **MAGIC** cloud-hopping method. Monkey was feeling confident. He surged past stars, galaxies and on through the blackness of space. Finally, he reached the edge of everything. There, he found five pillars. Whipping out a brush and ink, he scrawled **MONKEY WUZ 'ERE**. Then he went back to the Buddha.

"Done?" asked the Buddha.
"Easy-peasy!" boasted Monkey.

"Think again, Sun Wukong," replied his Eternal Greatness as he closed his hand gently around the puffed-up primate. There, in a WRINKLE of the Buddha's palm, Sun Wukong saw the Five Pillars with his graffiti on them. He felt a little smaller than he had before. "Why don't you try again?" suggested the Buddha, kindly. Monkey tried and tried, but no matter where he went he could never leave the Buddha's hand, because Monkey was of this universe, whereas the Supremo is of all creation.

Tiring of the game, Buddha realized that the maniac monkey would never learn this particular lesson. He took the self-proclaimed Great Sage Equal to Heaven and buried his head under a MOUNTAIN. Maybe 500 years of "time out" would teach him. Then again, given Monkey's past record, maybe it wouldn't!

RAMA ~~AND~~
SITA

DEAR READERS
Write to me to tell me the things that are worrying you and I will do my best to advise you. No problem is too small.
YOUR ~~AGONY~~ ~~AUNT,~~ VALMIKI

DEAR AUNT VALMIKI
I've been carried off by a fearsome demon with ten heads. It happened when my hunky hubby Rama was out hunting with Lakshmana, his brother.

Laksh had drawn a magic circle around me for protection, but I stepped out of it when an old man came to the door for water. The trickster changed shape and flew off with me but luckily I managed to drop some jewels along the way.
SITA

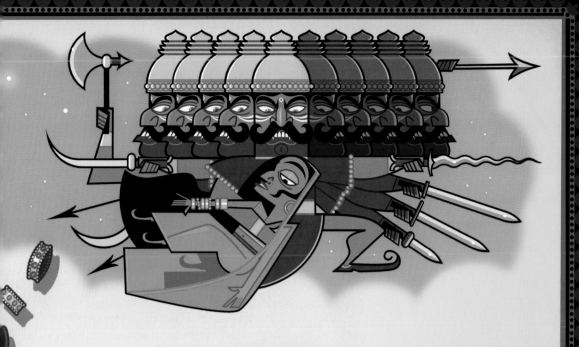

DEAR SITA

How awful! Ten heads? That will be the demon
Ravana. He is a real bad bean.

Your good nature has been your undoing.
If you'd stayed in Lakshmana's magic circle you'd be fine.
Leaving a trail was quick thinking, though. I hope your husband is
as smart as you and tracks you down soon.

YOUR AGONY AUNT, VALMIKI

DEAR AUNT VALMIKI

My wife has been kidnapped by a
horrid demon. I am in a terrible state
and have not slept for days.
Yours in agony

RAMA

PULL YOURSELF TOGETHER, RAMA!
Don't you know a husband's duty is to look after his wife?
There's only one thing you can do. You must rescue her, duh!
Start immediately – there's no time to waste!
VALMIKI

DEAR AUNT VALMIKI
I am kept a prisoner in Ravana's island fortress, Lanka,
guarded by fierce demons.

Trijata, one of Ravana's wives, dreamed that Rama came with an army
and destroyed Lanka. I'd rather die than cause suffering.

The days turn into weeks and there is no sign of my fella. Where is he?
I met a strange monkey in the garden. He whispered that Rama will
come. Am I losing my mind? I am so sad, I can't bear it. Sniff.
SITA

MY SWEET SITA
Hang on in there, girl. Your visitor was Hanuman, King of
the Monkeys. If he's on Rama's side, everything will be OK.
Be patient just a little longer.
YOUR CARING VALMIKI

DEAR AUNT VALMIKI

I raised an army of the roughest, toughest monkeys, but then
I hit a glitch. Lanka is an island – and my troops can't swim.
We were stuck for months!

Our luck turned when I started firing arrows into the sea out of
sheer boredom. The fish complained to their god Varuna and he
struck a bargain – he promised to hold up a bridge if I stopped firing
at the fish. Genius! War is on the menu again!

THE GREATEST RAMA

DEAR RAMA

– Whatever

V

DEER VLAK VALMIKI
I WO Z HAVIN A LUVLY SLEEP WEN RAVANAZ BOYS WOK ME. THEY WANT ME TO FITE RAMA. RAV IZ MY BRUVA, BUT I FINK HE WOZ RONG TO STEEL RAMAS WIFE. WOT SHUD I DO?
KUMBY

DEAR HANUMAN
You never fail to make me laugh, you cheeky monkey! Only one thing can kill Ravana – a special arrow hidden somewhere inside his palace. Good luck!
VALMIKI

DEAR KUMBHAKARNA
What a fine giant you are! You see that Ravana did wrong, but you want to be loyal. I think you should fight alongside your elder brother, even if means dying.
AUNTY VALMIKI

P.S.: Try inside the Crystal Pillar...

DEAR AUNT VALMIKI
I am a peaceful hermit monkey who lives in the distant hills and I definitely don't like wars. But what would be the best way to kill an invincible demon with ten heads?
Yours peacefully
H

DEAR AUNTY

Rama may be a big hero but he's also a monumental wally. He's just spent years fighting to get me back, spilling rivers of blood, and causing torrents of tears. Now he looks at me coldly and says, "Do what you want and go where you want."

I don't understand! I've spent all this time dreaming of being back together. I wish I could die! I did try. I built a funeral pyre and jumped on, but the flames wouldn't touch me. Yours miserably,

SITA

DEAR SITA

You truly are a good and pure person.
I wish I could say the same about your
husband. I think he is envious of the
time you spent with Ravana.
Give him time.

YOUR LOVING AUNT

P.S. This is such a great story, I'll
have to write it down one day.

DEAR VALMIKI

I took Sita home and made her my queen.
It was wonderful for a bit, but then I began to
think people were laughing at me and saying
that Sita preferred Ravana to me. So I told
Laksh to take Sita to the forest and kill her.
Oh, what have I done?

RAMA

OH FOR GOODNESS SAKE, RAMA!

Grow up! It doesn't matter what people
think. Here's what to do – release your
fanciest white horse and let it roam through
your lands. Most won't touch it because it
belongs to you, but someone will...

V

DEAR AUNT V

I did as you said – and wouldn't you know it –
Sita's two sons stopped my horse in the forest.
Sita is alive – good old Laksh didn't kill her after
all! I begged Sita to come back, but she said
she couldn't face being hurt by me again. As I
watched, the fire god Agni appeared to take Sita
home to Goddess Mother Earth. What a fool I've
been! I am dedicating my life to love, harmony
and the memory of Sita. Peace!

RAMA

DEAR RAMA
Now you're learning!
VALMIKI x

MOMOTARO THE PEACH BOY

A WASHERWOMAN and her husband lived by the endlessly flowing river. They worked hard and enjoyed life, but they never had a child. Together they grew a little **OLDER** and a little slower. They became known as Obaasan (Granny) and Ojiisan (Grandpa).

One day, while up to her elbows in soapsuds, Obaasan noticed a box floating downstream. She hooked it out of the water and found an enormous **PEACH** inside. "What a stroke of luck," she smiled. "I'll surprise Ojiisan with a peach for supper." And she took it home. Ojiisan really did get a **SURPRISE**! Just as he was about to cut into the peach, it spoke: "Wait!" Then the peach split in two, revealing a baby boy where the stone should have been. He was a real peach to be sure – chubby and chuckling in his birthday suit. The doddery duo called him **MOMOTARO**, which means Peach Boy.

Momotaro grew up big and strong. With his good looks and happy-go-lucky nature, it was impossible not to like him. But the Peach Boy was **LAZY**, too – he lay about reading books and taking naps.

He must have been busy **DREAMING** and planning adventures, though, because one day he calmly announced that he was off to defeat the Oni and bring back their treasure.

Who were the Oni? Only the most **TERRIFYING** monsters in the whole of Japan! Poor Obaasan and Ojiisan were horrified. Ojiisan asked who would look after them if Momo went and got himself killed... then he called Momo a good-for-nothing son-of-a-peach... and then he said that he was **SORRY**, he didn't mean any of it, and he might even have an old sword somewhere. Everyone cried, hugged, and cried again. Obaasan made Momo's favourite dumplings and everyone hugged and cried some more. Parting was very hard.

The Peach Boy set off for the Island of the Oni with no clear idea where it was. He walked for miles across fields and forests. Whenever he was hungry, he stopped and had a dumpling – and if anyone joined him, he happily shared his snacks. This is how he ended up with his **FAITHFUL** companions: Mr Dog, Mr Monkey, and Miss Pheasant. The crew crossed to Oni Island in a tiny boat and by the time they got there, they were ready to **RUMBLE**!

You don't mess with the monstrous Oni. Close up, they have **WILD** hair, **WILD** claws, and **WILD** horns growing out of their heads. They make your legs turn to **JELLY**. But not the Great General Momotaro, of course! Momo, Mr Monkey, and Mr Dog fell upon the ogres, while Miss Pheasant flew at them from on high. The big **BULLIES** were completely taken by surprise. When it was all over, brave Momotaro lined up the defeated Oni and made them promise to be good.

Oh what a hoard of **TREASURE** the victors found! Kimonos from Kyoto, opals from Osaka, tea from Tokyo, and sapphires from Sapporo. After sharing the **LOOT**, Momotaro went back to Obaasan and Ojiisan, looked after them, and they all lived happily ever after.

WARNING: THIS BRO-MANCE GETS A BIT SOPPY.

GILGAMESH ~~AND~~ ENKIDU

THIS IS AN EPIC TALE. Like all the best stories, it's got everything that matters most – fighting, fame, fun, and **FRIENDSHIP**. There are even a few personal grooming tips thrown in! It is the tale of two pals who were made for each other.

First, meet **GILGAMESH**, King of Uruk. He is a tall, muscled young man who boasts all his teeth (no mean feat in the days before toothbrushes and toothpaste!). With his oiled-back hair and glossy beard, he's as dashing as they come.

HOW DO YOU MAKE A GILGAMESH?

Take two parts "god" and mix with one part "human". Decorate with devastating good looks, then add a dash of fame and the irresistible whiff of **VICTORY** in battle. Sounds pretty perfect, huh? Well, 'Mesh did have a few flaws. He was restless by nature and had trouble seeing people as equals. He was also prone to going to war at the slightest offence.
In short, he was a **BAD KING**.

'Mesh always returned from battle without a scratch, but thousands of his young soldiers weren't so lucky. And while mothers **MOURNED** their sons, 'Mesh had glorious monuments and palaces built to celebrate his victories. He drove his people hard, and wore them out with work and war. At night, his subjects **PRAYED** to their gods for a kinder king.

The goddess Aruru heard the people's cries. Endlessly wise, she saw what Gilgamesh needed – a **FRIEND**. She set about making Enkidu.

HOW DO YOU MAKE AN ENKIDU?

Take a fistful of muddy clay – about two parts "beast" and one part "human". Pinch it between thumb and forefinger, then roll it about in all the dustballs and hair on the floor. Then leave to set in the sun and rain – it's **ROUGH** but it's ready!

Aruru set her fierce creation loose. **ENKIDU** was brand new, like the very first man and he had a lot to learn. He tried eating the messy remains of rotting animals – like jackals do – but it made him sick. He tried nibbling grass – like deer do – but it wasn't exactly tasty. He settled on digging for grubs with his fingernails until he found a source of **READY MEALS** – animals that had been caught in hunters' traps.

Enkidu was thirsty, so he went down to the river and drank. On the opposite bank sat a **HUNTER**, watching him with hatred and fear. She was tired of finding her traps sprung and empty. This rugged woman had spent entire seasons outdoors, but she had never seen anything like Enkidu. He was to blame for her smashed-up traps, but he was too **WILD** for her to face. Only one person could handle this beast...

Gilgamesh was staring out of the window watching his newest palace take shape. Tens of thousands of labourers swarmed over the half-built walls, and even at this distance he could hear the sharp crack of the whips. The stonemasons at work on his statue looked like tiny ants. This one was going to look **AWESOME**!

'Mesh was only half-listening to a simple hunter, who'd come bellyaching about her boring country problems. Suddenly, one word made him perk up. "A **WILDMAN**, you say?" he began. "Yes, your majesty. A shaggy-haired wolf boy. Breaking my traps," complained the hunter. "Then **TAME** him," advised King Gilgamesh. "Choose the prettiest girl from the Temple of Ishtar – she'll help you."

And that was how **SHAMHAT** found herself heading into the country with the hunter. The two women were close in age but looked like different species! One had lived in **LUXURY** and had skin like cream; the other's skin was like a tough old boot!

The next time Enkidu came down to the river, he sniffed suspiciously. There was something **DIFFERENT** about the air. Then he saw Shamhat combing her hair. She sensed his stare, but pretended not to notice. **CRIKEY**! He was beastly alright – huge, hairy and smelling like old cheese! Enkidu moved closer. If Shamhat was afraid, she didn't show it. "Come," she said softly. "Let's get you cleaned up."

After a week with Shamhat, Enkidu had lost his animal **PONG**. For the first time he had tasted cooked food, felt the warmth of a fire, and slept under cosy blankets. He listened as Shamhat described life in the temple, the great city of Uruk, and its mighty king...

Uh oh! Bad idea. Enkidu pointed towards Uruk. "Me **FIGHT** Gilgamesh," he grunted.

Gilgamesh soon heard the rumours: the beast-boy was coming for him. They met on the plains outside the city. Without a word, they **SMACKED** into each other. The heavens shook and the ground rocked. Enkidu wrapped his arms around Gilgamesh, just as the bears had shown him. He dug his toenails into the dirt, just as the stags had taught him, and pushed with all his might. But Gilgamesh did not budge!

'Mesh had never known such raw power. This guy was **AWESOME**! The king dropped his shoulder and quickly shifted his weight, just like he'd been taught. Your average bruiser would have gone over like a sack of breadsticks, but not Enkidu. Sure, he lost his balance – but he brought down Gilgamesh with him! **KABLAM**! It was no good – made for each other by the gods, the two were a perfect match!

Something **ODD** was happening to 'Mesh's face. He felt it wrinkle and the corners of his mouth pull up. He was smiling! The shaggy one was grinning from ear to ear, too. It wasn't a wrestling hold anymore. This was a **HUG**! 'Mesh and Enkidu stood together on the plain, hugging, and laughing like loonies!

A World of
Myths &
Legends

THE CLASSICAL WORLD

Greek and Roman myths are some of the oldest stories of the Western world. These are tales of gods and monsters – where people get to fly around in magic sandals and behave really, really terribly.

GREECE AND ROME

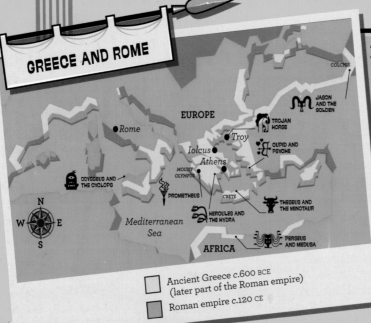

COLCHIS

EUROPE

JASON AND THE GOLDEN

Rome

Troy

TROJAN HORSE

Iolcus

CUPID AND PSYCHE

Athens

MOUNT OLYMPUS

ODYSSEUS AND THE CYCLOPS

PROMETHEUS

CRETE

THESEUS AND THE MINOTAUR

HERCULES AND THE HYDRA

Mediterranean Sea

PERSEUS AND MEDUSA

AFRICA

N W E S

Ancient Greece c.600 BCE
(later part of the Roman empire)

Roman empire c.120 CE

LANDS AND PEOPLE

"**CLASSICAL**" describes ancient Greek or Roman times. Greek civilization was at its height from around 800 to 300 BCE. The Romans rose to power a bit later – around 2,000 years ago. Their empire stretched across three continents.

COPY CATS

The all-conquering Romans were super-keen on the Greeks' stories, especially the ones about gods, warriors, and monsters. They stole the best characters and, if they could be bothered, they changed the gods' names to make them sound more Roman!

~~ZEUS~~
JUPITER

~~HERMES~~
MERCURY

TELLING TALES

Classical myths were written down by famous poets, playwrights and historians, such as Homer, Hesiod, Plutarch, and Sophocles. We owe the tales of Troy's heroes to the Greek poet Homer, working around 700 BCE, and Roman poet Virgil, writing around 80 CE.

HOMER

DID YOU KNOW?

WE STILL CONNECT WITH GREEK MYTHS. A HUGE JOB IS CALLED A "HERCULEAN TASK" AFTER THE 12 LABOURS OF THE HERO HERCULES. "TROJAN HORSES" ARE VIRUSES THAT SNEAK INSIDE OUR COMPUTERS, JUST LIKE THE MYTHICAL WOODEN HORSE SENT INTO TROY AS A FAKE PEACE OFFERING.

Replica of the Trojan Horse

FIGHTING TALK

Classical Greece was made up of small city-states. These were constantly squabbling with each other or banding together to fight invaders from the East. Perhaps that's why the Greeks had so many stories about heroes fighting and generally being epic! Some tales were based on real events, like the ones about the Trojan War.

THE MYTHS

Greek gods were supreme beings who just couldn't help poking their noses into human business and stirring things up. They lived on Mount Olympus – a real place – but only after they had first won an almighty battle against an older generation of gods, the Titans.

Heroes were the gods' half-human offspring, blessed with super powers. We've met Theseus, Perseus, Jason, super-strong Hercules, and wily Odysseus. We've also heard the story of Psyche – a rare female heroine – who was rewarded for her struggles by being allowed to become a god.

Greek vase showing soldiers preparing to go off to war

Coin showing Zeus, king of the Greek gods

EUROPE

When Rome collapsed in the 400s CE, Europe was plunged into the "Dark Ages". New gods and myths replaced the old classical ones, heralding from Germanic tribes in the West and Slavic peoples in the East.

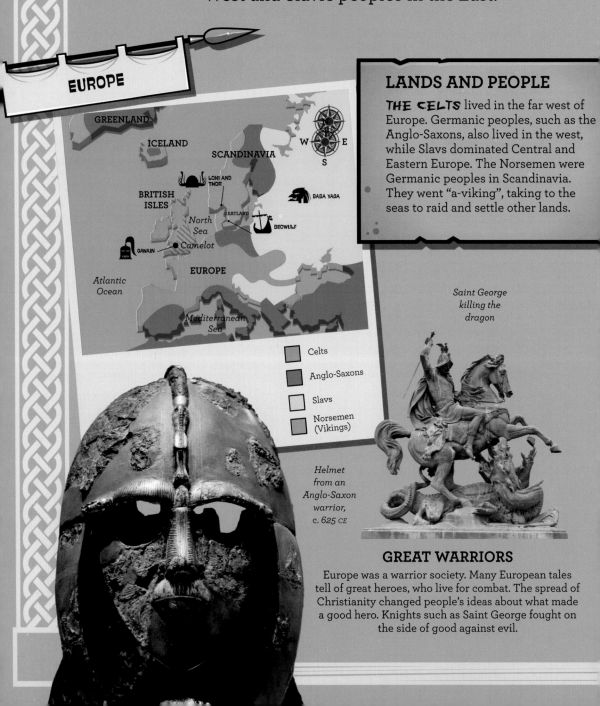

EUROPE

GREENLAND

ICELAND

SCANDINAVIA

LOKI AND THOR

BRITISH ISLES

BABA YAGA

GEATLAND

North Sea

BEOWULF

GAWAIN

Camelot

EUROPE

Atlantic Ocean

Mediterranean Sea

Celts

Anglo-Saxons

Slavs

Norsemen (Vikings)

Helmet from an Anglo-Saxon warrior, c. 625 CE

LANDS AND PEOPLE

THE CELTS lived in the far west of Europe. Germanic peoples, such as the Anglo-Saxons, also lived in the west, while Slavs dominated Central and Eastern Europe. The Norsemen were Germanic peoples in Scandinavia. They went "a-viking", taking to the seas to raid and settle other lands.

Saint George killing the dragon

GREAT WARRIORS

Europe was a warrior society. Many European tales tell of great heroes, who live for combat. The spread of Christianity changed people's ideas about what made a good hero. Knights such as Saint George fought on the side of good against evil.

TELLING TALES

Myths were usually passed on by word of mouth – people whiled away long evenings by the fire telling stories that often mixed fact and fiction. In the 1200s, an Icelander called Snorri Sturluson wrote a history of Viking kings – but as well as covering real figures, it told of gods and goddesses, too!

Viking bedpost carved into the shape of a mythical beast

A copy of Snorri Sturluson's manuscript, the Prose Edda

FANTASY FIGURES

European stories were full of fantastical creatures – fire-breathing dragons, unicorns, frost giants, goblins, werewolves, swamp monsters, demons, witches, and vampires. People just loved spooking each other out! In their thrilling tales, the forces of nature were imagined as terrifying spirits.

THE MYTHS

Full of enchantments and bewitchings, some of the world's most famous tales come from Europe. They contain violent battles, dangerous voyages and horrifying monsters.

In this small pick of European legends, we've met slippery Loki and his brother Thor and followed the exploits of beefy Beowulf, a fearless Germanic prince. We've met one of the (mostly!) brave knights of Arthur's Round Table, and we've also encounter Baba Yaga, the scariest witch of European folklore.

Arthur, King of the Knights of the Round Table

DID YOU KNOW?

THE VIKINGS BELIEVED THAT THERE WERE NINE DIFFERENT WORLDS IN THE UNIVERSE, EACH INHABITED BY A DIFFERENT KIND OF BEING. THE REALM OF HUMANS WAS CALLED MIDGARD, WHILE THE SKY GODS LIVED IN ASGARD. THE MAIN SKY GODS WERE ODIN, THOR, FREY, AND FREYA.

Viking pendant showing the goddess Freya

AFRICA

Africa's dazzling variety of peoples all have one thing in common – they love a good story! Traditional storytellers often begin their tales with cunning phrases that catch people's attention and make them settle down to listen.

LANDS AND PEOPLE

BIRTHPLACE of the human race, the vast continent of Africa stretches from the deserts of the north, through tropical rainforests to the southern grasslands. It is home to more than a billion people, who between them speak more than 1,000 different languages.

AFRICA

Mediterranean
Sea

SAHARA
DESERT

ANCIENT
EGYPT

OSIRIS
AND SET

AFRICA

ANANSI

YORUBA

CONGO
RAINFOREST

BLACKSMITH'S
FIX

Atlantic
Ocean

LEOPARD
AND DOG

Indian
Ocean

KALAHARI
DESERT

N W E S

Statue of Isis, the Egyptian goddess whose tears made the Nile flood

ISIS

Staff used by Yoruba people dancing to the god of storms (West Africa)

EVERYDAY WORRIES

Ancient Egyptian stories are obsessed with whether the Nile river will flood and fertilize the fields. Tales from the tropical zones tell of dangers in the deep forests. In areas that had strong kingdoms, stories show ordinary folk outwitting brutal kings. Other tales, meanwhile, explain the creation of the world.

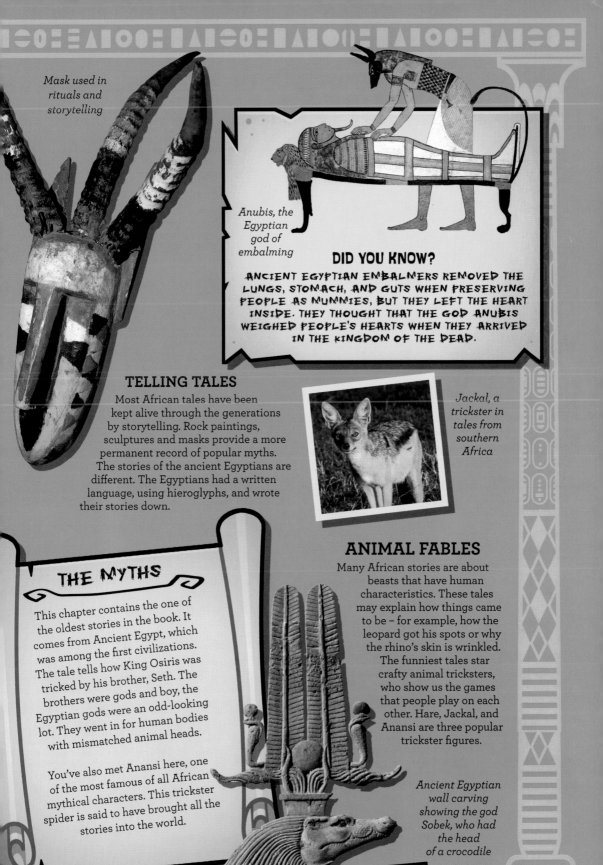

Mask used in rituals and storytelling

Anubis, the Egyptian god of embalming

DID YOU KNOW?

ANCIENT EGYPTIAN EMBALMERS REMOVED THE LUNGS, STOMACH, AND GUTS WHEN PRESERVING PEOPLE AS MUMMIES, BUT THEY LEFT THE HEART INSIDE. THEY THOUGHT THAT THE GOD ANUBIS WEIGHED PEOPLE'S HEARTS WHEN THEY ARRIVED IN THE KINGDOM OF THE DEAD.

TELLING TALES

Most African tales have been kept alive through the generations by storytelling. Rock paintings, sculptures and masks provide a more permanent record of popular myths. The stories of the ancient Egyptians are different. The Egyptians had a written language, using hieroglyphs, and wrote their stories down.

Jackal, a trickster in tales from southern Africa

THE MYTHS

This chapter contains the one of the oldest stories in the book. It comes from Ancient Egypt, which was among the first civilizations. The tale tells how King Osiris was tricked by his brother, Seth. The brothers were gods and boy, the Egyptian gods were an odd-looking lot. They went in for human bodies with mismatched animal heads.

You've also met Anansi here, one of the most famous of all African mythical characters. This trickster spider is said to have brought all the stories into the world.

ANIMAL FABLES

Many African stories are about beasts that have human characteristics. These tales may explain how things came to be – for example, how the leopard got his spots or why the rhino's skin is wrinkled. The funniest tales star crafty animal tricksters, who show us the games that people play on each other. Hare, Jackal, and Anansi are three popular trickster figures.

Ancient Egyptian wall carving showing the god Sobek, who had the head of a crocodile

SOBEK

CENTRAL AND SOUTH AMERICA

Maya... Aztecs... Incas... Central and South America have had their share of fantastic civilizations, each with their own magnificent myths. Of course, the region isn't just about ancient cultures – today, it's home to a rich mix of people.

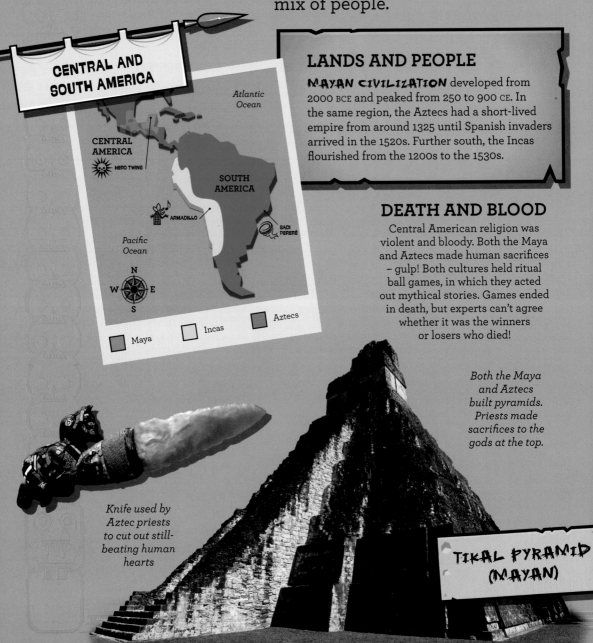

CENTRAL AND SOUTH AMERICA

Atlantic Ocean

CENTRAL AMERICA

HERO TWINS

SOUTH AMERICA

ARMADILLO

Pacific Ocean

SACI PERERÊ

N
W · E
S

☐ Maya   ☐ Incas   ☐ Aztecs

LANDS AND PEOPLE

MAYAN CIVILIZATION developed from 2000 BCE and peaked from 250 to 900 CE. In the same region, the Aztecs had a short-lived empire from around 1325 until Spanish invaders arrived in the 1520s. Further south, the Incas flourished from the 1200s to the 1530s.

DEATH AND BLOOD

Central American religion was violent and bloody. Both the Maya and Aztecs made human sacrifices – gulp! Both cultures held ritual ball games, in which they acted out mythical stories. Games ended in death, but experts can't agree whether it was the winners or losers who died!

Both the Maya and Aztecs built pyramids. Priests made sacrifices to the gods at the top.

Knife used by Aztec priests to cut out still-beating human hearts

TIKAL PYRAMID (MAYAN)

BOOKS OF BLOOD

The Maya may have been bloodthirsty, but they were cultured, too – and they loved writing down their discoveries and stories. Some Mayan books survive to this day. They tell us lots about Mayan gods and heroes.

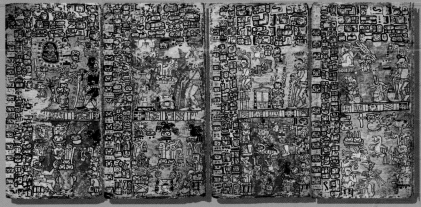

Mayan writing is in picture symbols, called hieroglyphs.

NATTY KNOTS

The Incas didn't have writing – they kept records on objects called *quipus*, which were elaborate systems of knotted strings. If it weren't for the detailed descriptions written down by the Spanish conquistadores (conquerors), we'd probably know hardly anything about Inca culture.

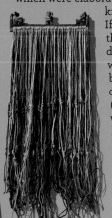

The quipu *is made of cotton cords or llama-hair string.*

THE MYTHS

The Maya, Aztecs and other peoples of Central America worshipped many gods. The main Aztec god was Quetzalcoatl, a dude who was half-rattlesnake and half-quetzal bird. In the Mayan story of the Hero Twins, you've met some characters with equally crazy names and weird habits!

Today, the region is home to people from many backgrounds – descendants of the original inhabitants, plus people of European and African origin. This diversity is reflected in their stories – the Brazilian character Saci Pererê, for example, shares features with the chaos-bringing West African spirit, Eshu.

The Aztec plumed serpent god, Quetzalcoatl

QUETZALCOATL

DID YOU KNOW?

THE CONQUISTADORES WROTE REPORTS ON THE PEOPLE THEY FOUND IN CENTRAL AND SOUTH AMERICA. ONE DESCRIBED THE MONTH OF THE DEAD – A MONTH-LONG FEAST ENJOYED BY THE INCAS IN THE COMPANY OF DEAD, MUMMIFIED ANCESTORS. THE GUESTS MUST HAVE BEEN A BIT STIFF!

Inca mummy

ASIA

It almost seems unfair to select just a handful of stories from Asia – it's the world's largest continent and contains so many different peoples and cultures. Rest assured, though, the ones chosen for this book are real goodies!

LANDS AND PEOPLE

THE TALES here come from China, India, Japan, and ancient Mesopotamia. Some of the world's earliest civilisations arose in Asia – Mesopotamia, a fertile area in what is now Iraq, was a civilisation hotspot and had flourishing cities from around 4000 BCE.

Among the god Vishnu's ten avatars were lion-faced Narasimha, hero-boar Varaha, and Kurma, a turtle.

ANCIENT INDIA

Gods and spirits are key to most Asian tales, and there's no shortage of them. In India, the Hindu religion has thousands! Its gods get reincarnated over and over – often with a change of name and heart – so it's hard to keep track!

NARASIMHA   VARAHA   KURM

Stone tablet inscribed with the Epic of Gilgamesh

WRITTEN IN STONE

Gilgamesh, an epic from Mesopotamia, is the world's oldest written story. Carved into stone tablets around 2150 BCE, the tale itself was even older. It tells of heroic King Gilgamesh, his wild best friend and their even wilder adventures. The Mesopotamians also had a bunch of gods. The most important two – Baal the Rainmaker and Yam, god of chaos – were locked in eternal battle.

Chinese vases often feature images from myths, such as dragons.

THE MYTHS

They say an infinite number of monkeys bashing away on typewriters would eventually write the works of Shakespeare – but not even an infinite number of Shakespeares would come up with the story of Monkey! Its "hero" is bigheaded, selfish, quick-tempered, unpredictable, and so infuriating that he even makes the wise Jade Emperor lose his legendary cool! You'll find part of his story here.

You've also met cute Momotaro, who takes on some monstrous Japanese ogres, epic King Gilgamesh, and Rama and Sita, stars of the greatest Indian story of all time, the Ramayana.

Japanese carving print showing an oni (ogre).

ANCIENT CHINA

Today, China is the most populous country in the world. It has an ancient history and its early stories were written down more than 2,000 years ago. Some explain how the world came into being; others star fantastical dragons, phoenixes or other crazy creatures. The stories are a heady mix of Taoist, Buddhist, and Confucianist beliefs and teachings.

OCEANIA

Two of our tales come from Oceania, the part of the world that is made up of Australia, New Zealand and countless Pacific islands. These scattered lands have many traditions, many peoples – and many, many stories.

OCEANIA

LANDS AND PEOPLE

PEOPLE first came to Oceania from Asia during the last Ice Age, more than 50,000 years ago. They were the Aboriginal Australians. Between 3,000 and 7,000 years ago, there were waves of new arrivals. They spread through Oceania, island-hopping in canoes.

MICRONESIA

SOLOMON ISLANDS

POLYNESIA

MELANESIA

ULURU (AYER'S ROCK) RAINBOW SERPENT

Pacific Ocean

AUSTRALIA

NEW ZEALAND

MAUI HAWAIIAN ISLANDS

N W E S

ULURU

Traditionally, the Aboriginal Australians lived as hunter-gatherers.

SACRED STORIES

Each Aboriginal Australian tribe had its own version of the Dreaming – the story of how life was created. You must be careful when telling a Dreamtime story because some people don't like their Dreaming being passed on. Don't worry, though – it's fine to retell the story of the Wawilak sisters (pages 134–141).

Dreamtime stories tell of how the ancestors formed every feature of the land – including the amazing rock formation Uluru (also known as Ayer's Rock).

Nguzu nguzu *(protective figurehead)* from a canoe in the Solomon Islands

Aboriginal rock art, Kakadu, Australia

TELLING TALES

The people of Oceania didn't write their myths down. They passed them on from generation to generation by endlessly retelling them in stories and dance. Aboriginal people also drew figures from myths on bark and on rocks scattered around the landscape.

ISLAND CULTURE

On the Pacific islands of Melanesia, Micronesia and Polynesia, people tell tales of quarrels, bravery, and sacrifice. These islanders traditionally made their living by fishing, and blamed angry gods for storms that wrecked their ships. They also often went to war with people from neighbouring islands.

Polynesian dancers

THE MYTHS

In Aboriginal stories, one of the most important figures is the Rainbow Serpent, which brings the rain and guards the waterholes. Dreamings are mythological tales that stretch across the land in a web of ancient tracks and trails.

The seafaring peoples of Melanesia, Micronesia and Polynesia are very different to each other, but share similar stories – often about how their islands were created. Both they, and the Aboriginal Australians tell stories about how the spirits of their ancestors walk the land today.

Jade pendants shaped like the hook Maui used to fish up the Pacific islands

INDEX

PHOTOGRAPHIC CREDITS

THE PUBLISHER WOULD LIKE TO THANK THE FOLLOWING FOR THEIR KIND PERMISSION TO REPRODUCE THEIR IMAGES:

l=left, r=right, tl=top left, tc=top centre, tr=top right, cl=centre left, c=centre, cr=centre right, b=bottom, bl=bottom left, bc=bottom centre, br=bottom right

ALAMY: 212bl (David Lyons), 212br (David Robertson), 213tr (Ivy Close Images), 213cl (David Robertson), 213bl (Heritage Image Partnership Ltd), 213br (Holmes Garden Photos), 214bl (The Art Archive), 214br (Heritage Image Partnership Ltd), 215tl (Eddie Gerald), 215tr (Stock Connection Blue), 215cr (SuperStock), 221bl (Stuart Pearce), 221br (Heritage Image Partnership Ltd), 217bl (Heritage Image Partnership Ltd), 217br (Ricardo Ribas), 218b (Louise Batalla Duran), 219tl (World History Archive), 219tr (www.BibleLandPictures.com); **CORBIS:** 68 (Werner Forman), 211br (Hoberman Collection); **GETTY IMAGES:** 215b (DEA/G Sioen), 220bl (Marquicio Pagola), 221tl (Werner Forman), 216cr (Shaun Curry/Stringer), 217t (Universal History Archive), 217cr (Werner Forman); **SHUTTERSTOCK:** All other images.